CROSSFIRE

Love & Lies Book 1

Alex Strong

Red Dahlia Publishing

CROSSFIRE

Copyright © 2015 Alex Strong

This book is a work of fiction. Names, characters, and events are the product of the author's imagination. Any resemblances to actual persons, living or dead, or events is coincidental.

Cover Art © konradbak/BortN66/fotolia
Cover Design by J.P. Irons

ISBN: 978-0-9913614-5-8

I dedicate this book to my friend Cattigan for making me feel like a rock star.

CHAPTER ONE

Jillian Sandro's hand tightened around the cell phone pressed hard against her ear as she listened to the message. Another job rejection.

She deleted the message and dialed a number that went immediately to voice mail.

"Cameron," she said into the phone, fighting back tears of frustration, "I don't know what you're telling these people, but you need to stop. This is my career you're screwing with!"

Jillian ended the call and slammed the phone on her dresser, instantly regretting it. She couldn't afford a new phone if this one broke.

After checking to see that it had survived the abuse, she strapped on her iPod and headed out for a much needed run.

Music blasted through the headphones and anger consumed her thoughts as Jillian started jogging down the sidewalk from her father's Renton home. Looking over her shoulder for vehicles turning into the suburban development, she mis-judged her stride off the curb, causing her ankle to roll.

"Dammit," she cried out, falling back onto the curb in pain and embarrassment.

"Are you all right?" someone asked.

Jillian looked up into the brightest blue eyes she had ever seen.

"Um, yeah, I think it's fine," she said to the tall stranger who had appeared from nowhere. He was holding a leash with a German shepherd on the other end of it.

"Here," he said, "let me help you up."

Before she could protest, he took her hand and put an arm around her.

"You know, I'm sure if I just walk it off, I'll be fine." She tried to take a step away from him, but as soon as she put her weight on the left foot, pain shot through the ankle, causing her to lose balance and start to fall. He caught her, and Jillian could feel the heat rising to her cheeks as she stood there, propped up by his solid arms.

"I don't think you're going to be able to walk this off," said the beautiful stranger. "Is there somewhere nearby I could help you get to?"

She sighed. So much for the therapeutic run.

"I'm just down the street," she said, pointing.

He looked where she indicated, squinting his eyes. "Didn't make it very far, did you?" he said.

"This should be a piece of cake."

Before she could decide what he meant by that, he handed the leash to his dog, who clamped it in its mouth, and swept her up.

"This really isn't necessary," she stammered. "My other foot is fine, I'm sure I could hobble home."

"I know," he said, looking straight ahead which she was grateful for. Jillian was afraid she might burst into flames if she had to look into his eyes at this close proximity. "But it will be quicker. Now, which house is it?"

"Fifteen forty-two," she mumbled.

"Not far at all," he said, only slightly breathless.

God, this was embarrassing. Jillian wondered if her cheeks could get any hotter. She caught a whiff of his aftershave and involuntarily inhaled, trying to breathe in more of it.

"You okay?" he asked, looking concerned.

"Um, yeah." Surely steam was coming off her by now.

She glanced down at the dog, who was walking obediently next to them.

"Aren't you worried your dog is going to run away?" she asked.

"Nope."

It didn't take long, but to Jillian it felt like an eternity until he was setting her down on the front stoop.

"Thank you," she said.

"Glad I could help. I'm Reid, by the way. Reid Jackson. I live in that house." He pointed to the gray house across the street, two driveways down.

"Jillian Sandro."

"It's nice to meet you, Jillian."

He extended a hand that she reluctantly shook. She had made a fool of herself, and just wished he would leave her to climb inside a hole and feel like an idiot in private.

"I'm trained in first-aid," he said. "If you want, I could take a look at it."

"Oh, no," she said, shaking her head. "I'll be fine. I've had my share of twists and sprains. This is nothing. I just need to get inside and ice it. I'm sure I'll be fine."

"Do you need help getting inside?" he asked, looking a little dejected.

She started to feel bad. As embarrassed as she was, Jillian didn't want her neighbor, who was being so helpful, to think she was a complete bitch.

"Sure," she said, reaching out to him. "That would be great."

With Reid helping her to stand, Jillian slipped a key from her wristband and unlocked the door.

"Hold on," he said before they walked in.

She watched as he tied the dog's leash to the railing.

"Now you don't trust your dog to stay?" she asked.

"Not when I'm away," he said with a boyish

smile.

Reid assisted her to the couch, then took off to grab an ice pack from the nearby kitchen. Jillian watched the undeniably attractive neighbor dig through her freezer. Even his sandy blonde hair was mussed in a way that gave her heart a slight pause. And those bright blue eyes were to die for. She gave herself a mental slap. Guys this good looking were either taken or trouble—or both.

Reid buried his head in Jillian's freezer, but he wasn't finding any ice packs.

"Are you sure you have any in here?" he asked.

Her brows furrowed as she thought about it, and then those dark eyes went big. "Sorry, they're in the garage freezer, not that one."

"Is this the door?" he asked, heading towards the logical option and she nodded.

It didn't take long to find them. As he headed back into the house, Reid noticed a stack of boxes in the corner, some of them half-unpacked, or packed, depending on how you looked at it.

"There you go," he said, positioning the pack on her ankle.

"I can't thank you enough," she said, looking at him with those warm brown eyes. They were rimmed with thick dark lashes and matched the long hair, pulled back into a ponytail almost perfectly.

"It's nothing," he said. Reid looked around the

room. The decor was minimal and, if he had to guess, it had been put together by a male. There seemed to be very little female influence in here.

"How long have you lived here?" he asked.

"I've only been here for a couple weeks now."

That explained the boxes.

"I didn't realize anyone had moved onto the street so recently," he said.

"It's actually my dad's house," she said, lowering her eyes. "He's lived here a couple years now. I'm kind of," she paused, "in limbo at the moment. My dad is letting me stay with him until I can get back on my feet."

"I see."

"How about you?" Jillian asked, looking back up at him. "How long have you lived in the neighborhood?"

"It's been a couple years as well," he answered.

Reid's pocket started buzzing. He pulled out his phone to look at the screen, though he had no doubt who it was from.

"That would be work," he said. "Looks like I need to head out."

"What do you do?" she asked.

"I work with banking security systems," he said.

"Which bank?" she asked.

"I'm with an outside company," he explained. "I help install the systems and teach the banks how to use them. How about yourself?"

"I'm in—*was* in graphic design. Like I said, in limbo at the moment."

Reid nodded. "So are you okay here?" he asked.

"I'm fine," she said. "My dad should be home soon if I need anything."

"See you around, then," he said, heading for the door.

"Thank you," she called out, and he watched her blush for the umpteenth time. "In case I didn't say it already."

"No problem." he said, and left.

Reid flashed his badge at the guard and was waved into the parking lot for the building known by most people as the Alliance Security Systems offices. But Reid knew its true role as the headquarters for Section Four, one of five clandestine operations positioned in strategic locations of the continental United States.

He parked and walked to the only elevator in the lot, where he punched in his ten-digit code on the inside panel. Once the doors closed on him, a full body scan was performed before the lift made its way to the second floor. When he stepped off, Reid was immediately greeted by his partner and closest friend.

"Jackson, there you are," Aaron Wells said, looking at his watch. "Took you long enough."

Reid shook his head, choosing not to respond.

Aaron always gave him a hard time for being the last to arrive. As much as he loved his job, Reid purposely bought a house outside the city, just within the approved perimeter for operatives' primary residences. He didn't expect Aaron to understand that a little bit of distance was his coping mechanism.

"Had to drive the Camaro in," Aaron said, sitting on the corner of Reid's desk. "The bike was in pieces when I got the call."

"Anything wrong with it?" Reid asked while thumbing through some papers left on his desk.

"Nah, just giving it a tune-up."

And that was Aaron's coping mechanism. He and Reid both owned the same high-end bike, but while Reid wouldn't let anyone but the dealer touch it, Aaron was completely hands on.

"How about you?" Aaron asked. "In the middle of anything interesting?"

"Matter of fact, I was," said Reid. "Met a neighbor today."

Aaron rolled his eyes.

"A female neighbor."

Now Aaron's eyebrows went up in interest, but they were interrupted before either men could say anything else.

"Agent Jackson, Agent Wells," a woman barked. "Briefing room, now."

Both men followed Director Laura Rollins into the conference room and sat at the table where the rest of the team was already assembled.

Director Rollins made her way to the front where images were being projected on a smart screen.

"We just got word that the arms sale between Voichek and Polesun has been moved to tomorrow afternoon," she said. "We have to act fast if we are going to intercept the broker. No new information, just moving the timetable up. You have your mission. Now grab your gear and head over to Boeing Field. Wheels up in one hour."

Jillian was still icing her ankle on the couch when her father came home that afternoon.

"Jillian," he exclaimed. "What happened?"

The look on his weary face did not surprise her one bit. Jacob always worried too much when it came to his only daughter. With the rest of his family still in Italy, she was all he had.

"I fell today while I was out running," she said with a sheepish smile.

Jacob carefully lifted the ice pack off her swollen ankle.

"And you made it home on this?" he asked.

"No. A neighbor happened to be nearby and helped me in."

"Anyone I know?" he asked sternly. A stranger in their house with her would be even more worrisome than a running accident.

"I don't know," she said. "Reid Jackson? He lives just a few doors down."

Jillian watched her father frown and what she

thought was worry crossed his face, but then he shook his head.

"Doesn't sound familiar," said Jacob, moving towards the kitchen. "I'm afraid I haven't done a very good job of getting to know my neighbors."

"Anyway, he helped me in, got me an ice pack, and left."

"Do you think you'll see him again?" her father asked.

"I don't know," she said with a shrug. "He lives across the street, so I guess it's possible. Why?"

"No reason." Jacob rummaged through the pantry. "You should be more careful when you're running."

"Of course, Papa."

In the locker room Reid placed his personal items on the shelf of a locker and strapped on his side arms.

"So about this neighbor, this *female* neighbor," Aaron said as he strapped on his own weapons and Reid gave a half smile.

"I was walking Max," he told Aaron, "when a jogger fell and twisted her ankle. I helped her, and it turns out she lives across the street from me."

"Was she hot? She must be hot, or you wouldn't be bringing this up."

Reid shut his locker. "Yes, she happened to be attractive," he said, fighting the grin as he remembered her intoxicating eyes staring back at him not so long ago. "I didn't get a chance to talk much with her, though, before we got called in."

"Are you going to see her again?" asked Aaron.

"Seeing as how she's practically my next door neighbor," Reid said, "it's very likely."

"Just watch your step," Aaron said, slamming his own locker shut.

Reid frowned. "What are you talking about?"

"You know damn well what I'm talking about. Guys in our line of work don't do relationships. Fooling around is okay, but I think we both know that's not really your thing. It's bad enough you have a dog to worry about."

"Excuse me if I need something besides you to keep me company," Reid said defensively.

"Then a dog is perfect for that," said Aaron. "Dogs don't ask questions. Look man, I'm just thinking about your career. Your loyalty is part of what makes you so damn good at your job. But it could also be your undoing if you're not careful."

"I appreciate your concern, but you don't have to worry about me. I would never do anything to compromise my job or this team."

"Good," Aaron said as they made their way out of the locker room. "And that's why you're going to stay away from this neighbor."

"Whatever," Reid muttered. Aaron didn't know what he was talking about.

Four days later Reid was headed home and ready to pass out from exhaustion. The quick turnaround in Dubai was leaving him with serious jet lag, and yet he drove past his house and continued up the hill to the nearby grocery store. Max was in need of dog food, and Reid wanted to pick it up before he crawled into bed and crashed for the next several hours.

He picked up the forty-pound bag and carried it to the nearest open cashier. There was Jillian standing at the register. She looked up at him, appearing just as surprised as he was.

"Hi," she said, and he could see the color instantly rising to her cheeks.

"Hello," he said. "I didn't know you worked here."

The color deepened. "I just started a couple weeks ago."

"I see. How's your ankle?" he asked.

"Much better. I iced it that whole afternoon, and by the next day it felt fine. But I gave it another day just to be sure."

"Glad to hear it. Have you ran on it yet?" he asked.

"I did this morning before my shift. I made sure to keep my eye out for any curbs jumping out at me this time."

Reid laughed as he handed her the exact change. "That's always a good thing." He picked up his bag of dog food. "Well, I'm sure I'll see you around again," he said with a smile.

"Hey, um," she said, starting to blush again. Reid wasn't entirely sure if he found it embarrassing or flattering.

"I'm off in ten minutes. Would you like to grab—" she looked at her watch. "Would you like to grab some lunch with me?"

He was leaning more towards flattered.

"I would, but I really need to get home." Reid barely had the energy to make the short drive at this point. "Rain check?"

"Oh, yeah, sure."

Another customer started unloading their cart and Reid slipped away.

The next night Jillian was at the kitchen sink washing dishes when she thought she saw movement in the backyard. It was the second time that evening, and it made her uneasy. She walked over to the sliding door and switched on the light, but saw nothing unusual. She opened the door and called out to an imaginary cat, hoping that the sound of her voice would scare off any prowler that might be lurking in the shadows. Houses weren't often broken into in the neighborhood, but it still happened. She closed the door, making sure to lock it, then moved around the house and checked all the windows. A noise made her jump, but it was just someone across the street dragging their bins out to the curb.

"Crap," she muttered, remembering that

garbage needed to go out.

She walked out to the garage, stood by the bins, and chewed her nail, trying to decide whether or not to take it out. Realizing that in the morning she was going to feel like an idiot for being so paranoid, she hit the button and tried not to feel so exposed as the garage door rolled up its track. But as she dragged out the recycling bin, she couldn't shake the feeling that someone was watching her. She glanced down the street, wondering if Reid was home. Would he think she was being irrational? But as another shiver swept through her body, she started walking towards his house, glancing over her shoulder repeatedly.

Reid's front door loomed large before her as Jillian stepped up onto the porch. She knocked quietly and studied the swinging bench to her right while waiting. No movement could be heard inside. Perhaps no one was home. Or maybe she didn't knock hard enough. She raised her hand, debating whether to try again or just give it up, when the door opened. There was Reid, wearing only a pair of jeans and nothing else. For a second, Jillian forgot why she was standing there.

"Yes?" he asked when Jillian had still not found her tongue.

"Um, hi," she said. "I wasn't sure if you were home." She realized her hand was still raised in mid-knock and lowered it. "I wasn't sure if you were home," she repeated like an idiot. What was it about this man that made her brain turn to mush? Perhaps it was the incredible abs she was trying so hard to keep her eyes off of. "I just—" She started and then paused. "Damn, now I feel crazy saying this out loud."

Reid did nothing to help her out as she fumbled for the words. Didn't he realize how intimidating he was, standing there and studying her intently with his cool blue eyes? It was so unnerving.

"It's just that I can't shake the feeling that someone is watching me or something," she finally spilled out. "Twice I thought I saw something in my backyard. Maybe it's because I've never spent the night alone in this house before, but I was wondering if…" she started rubbing her forehead. "Well, I guess I don't know what I was going to ask you for. I'm sure I'm just being paranoid. So sorry for bothering you." She turned to leave.

"I could come take a look around," he said.

Jillian spun back around. "Really? I mean, if you don't mind, I think it would help me feel better. Even if it's just you telling me it's all in my head."

"Sure. Come in for a second and I'll grab my shirt and shoes."

She stepped in. Reid closed the door behind her and walked noiselessly down the hall. Now that she was standing in the relative safety of Reid's foyer, Jillian started to wonder if she *had* been imagining everything.

CHAPTER TWO

Reid ran upstairs to his room and Max lifted his head from where he had been sleeping on the floor.

"Some guard dog, you are," he said, grabbing the shirt he had just thrown on the foot of the bed. Another five minutes and he would have been tucked in for the night. He wondered if Jillian had actually been spooked, or if it was just an excuse to come talk to him. She did look worried.

Jillian was standing at the door where Reid had left her when he came back down the stairs. He grabbed his shoes from the closet and they headed out. He made sure to lock the door behind him.

"Where's your dad tonight?" he asked as they walked to her house.

"He had to go to Portland for work. He's only gone the one night."

"I see."

"I'm not normally this big a chicken," she said.

"I never said you were a chicken."

"I know. I just feel like one at the moment."

"Was the garage open when you left?" Reid asked.

"Shit," said Jillian. "I was bringing the garbage out and forgot to put it down before I came over."

"I'm sure it's fine. Let's go inside and take a look."

They walked into the house where nothing appeared to be disturbed and Jillian stood in the middle of the kitchen while Reid checked other doors and windows.

"I checked all those already," she said.

"Was the sliding door locked when you left?" he asked when it slid right open.

She frowned. "I could have sworn I did. I opened it to look outside and was sure I locked it. But maybe I forgot."

"Hmm…" Reid sensed she didn't believe she had forgotten. The door had a key lock that someone could have easily picked if they had the skill.

"Why don't you hang out here while I check the rooms upstairs?" he suggested.

She nodded and started chewing her thumbnail while Reid made his way up the stairs.

The first room he entered was the master

bedroom right off the top landing. It had two windows plus one in the bathroom, and all were closed and latched with no signs of forced entry. He found the same in the spare bedroom, and the hall bath only had skylights. Just to be thorough, Reid checked behind the shower curtain and found nothing but a few toiletries.

The last bedroom was Jillian's. More moving boxes were piled in a corner, some with contents spilling out, and Reid wondered if she was taking her time unpacking, or trying to not get too comfortable. He walked past a dresser with a few framed pictures. They were mostly pictures of Jillian and a woman who could only be her mother. Both had the same thick brown hair, olive skin, and chocolate colored eyes. He also noticed that Jillian couldn't have been more than fourteen or fifteen in the most recent of them.

After finding her window secure just like all the others, he rejoined Jillian downstairs in the kitchen.

"Everything seems to be in order upstairs," he said and saw her whole body relax.

"Thank you," she sighed and walked over to the counter where there was a half-empty bottle of red wine. "I could use a drink," she said, uncorking the bottle and reaching for a nearby glass. "Would you like some?"

"No thanks," he said, shaking his head. "I'm not much of a wine drinker."

"How about a beer?" she asked and moved over to the fridge. "I'm sure there's an IPA in here somewhere."

"That sounds good." Reid was sure there was no harm in accepting a beer from a neighbor.

Jillian pulled one out, found the bottle opener, and handed it to him before returning to where she'd left her glass of wine. Reid opted to simply lean against the counter next to the sink. He thought it best to keep at least a little distance between him and this…alluring neighbor. Aaron would be so proud of him.

"I can't decide if I'm relieved, or if I just feel like an idiot," she said.

"There's nothing wrong with being a little paranoid now and then." If Jillian knew half the crap Reid did, she would probably never sleep well again.

"So is there, um, a Mrs. Jackson upset that her husband had to go rescue a neighbor?" she asked without making eye contact with him.

Real subtle, thought Reid.

"No. I travel a lot for work which makes it harder to maintain relationships."

She nodded. "That makes sense."

But Reid couldn't resist.

"And what about you?" he asked. "Any guy out there jealous that you called on me instead of him?"

"Oh, I'm sure there are a few out there," she said with a sly smile. "But no one in particular."

Jillian polished off her wine, and Reid took another swig from his beer as he watched her walk towards him, her movement almost sensuous. Was it intentional?

She stopped at the sink next to where Reid was standing, rinsed out her glass, and turned to face him.

"I'm glad you were home tonight," she said quietly.

He faced her as he put his now empty bottle in the sink. His arm brushed against her soft bare skin. He let his hand rest on the counter, his fingertips just barely touching hers.

"Glad I could help," he said with a slight smile, wondering if it would be so wrong to kiss her right now.

He watched as her lips parted and was about to lean in when the house phone rang. Disappointment crossed Jillian's face as she walked over to answer it.

"Hello," she answered. "Yes, Papa, I remembered to take the garbage out." A pause and then she looked at Reid and smiled. "Yes, all the doors and windows are locked up tight. Okay, Papa, I love you too. Good night."

"I should probably get going," Reid said as she hung up the phone. Best to get out before he did anything he might regret later. "Thanks for the beer."

"Oh, okay," she said, following him to the front door. "Thanks for easing my fears."

"Don't forget to lock the door behind me."

She smirked. "Don't worry, I won't."

Reid was just about to step off the porch when he turned around before Jillian could close the door.

"Do you want to have dinner with me tomorrow night?" he asked, surprising himself. So much for making a clean escape. He could already hear Aaron telling him this wouldn't end well.

Jillian's eyes went big, clearly just as shocked by his request. Then she smiled.

"I would like that."

"Great," Reid said as a smile started to spread across his own face. "I'll pick you up at six."

"I will see you at six then," she said.

He turned around and walked home, wondering if he even remembered what it was like to go out on a date.

Reid knocked on Jillian's door promptly at six and she was ready to go. She had been ready for the past hour, nervously pacing the living room, desperately hoping her father didn't make it home before she left. She didn't like the idea of having to introduce the two yet, but knew her over-protective father would have insisted on it.

"Hi," Jillian said as she opened the door.

"Hello," said Reid.

She watched his eyes move up and down her body and hoped she had made the right wardrobe choice. Reid had not said where he would be taking her. She'd finally decided on a blue cotton sundress with a low-heeled sandal as the best bet.

[25]

"You look great," he said, and Jillian was relieved.

"Thanks. So do you." And she wasn't saying it just to return the compliment. He was wearing a lightweight button-down shirt with the sleeves rolled up, exposing his muscular forearms. It was untucked over a dark pair of fitted jeans.

"Shall we?" Reid asked.

Jillian grabbed her sweater and clutch from the bench next to the front door. It had been a warm late August day, but it would cool off quickly when the sun went down in a couple hours.

Reid's black Porsche Cayenne was at the end of her driveway, and he helped her into it before climbing into the passenger seat.

"So where are we headed?" she asked as Reid pulled out of the neighborhood.

"Have you ever eaten at the Dahlia Lounge downtown?"

She shook her head.

"Then it will be a first for the both of us," he said with a smile.

Jillian's heart fluttered. This was also her first date in a long time. She hoped she was ready for it.

"How did you decide on this place?" Jillian asked when they were seated in the downtown Seattle restaurant

"The owner, Tom Douglas, does a radio show that I catch from time to time. I've wanted to try this restaurant, but haven't had the opportunity until now."

"Is that the only reason you asked me out?" she teased. "So you could eat here without looking sad and lonely?"

Reid laughed and Jillian was immediately in love with the sound of it. It was so warm and sincere. She really needed to watch herself with this one.

"Something like that," he said. "And I thought it might be a good way for us to get to know each other. Seeing as how we're neighbors and all."

"Well, I'm always game for trying a new Tom Douglas restaurant," she said, opening the menu.

"You're familiar with him then?"

She nodded.

"Have you been to any of the others?"

"Just the sandwich shop down by Pike Place Market. I used to grab lunch from there all the time when I was working downtown."

Jillian could feel the smile melting from her own face as memories came flooding in. Reid gave a questioning look, but before he could say anything, she forced the smile back on and changed the subject.

"So where did you live before you moved into the neighborhood?" she asked. "Are you from the area?"

"I was in Seattle for about a year before Renton," he said. "And before that I was on the East Coast, where I grew up. How about you?"

Jillian sensed that he wasn't eager to talk much more about his upbringing.

"I've always lived in the area," she said. "I grew up in Renton, but moved into Seattle for school and was there until just recently."

Problem was that Jillian wasn't too eager to talk about her history either. Not yet at least. It was still too raw.

Fortunately they were saved from any more awkward questions by the server coming to tell them about the specials and take their drink orders.

"So how long have you been running?" Reid asked when the server stepped away, and Jillian was grateful. Here was a nice safe topic.

"I started running during college. The end of my freshman year to be exact."

"And what made you decide to take it up?"

Jillian blushed. "It was silly. You would laugh at me."

"What? No I won't."

She shook her head.

"You can't leave me hanging like this," he said.

Reid's bright blue eyes were staring right into hers and she sighed, forcing herself to look away.

"You've heard of the freshman fifteen, right?"

"Yes. Of course."

"I was a victim of the infamous curse," she said and his eyebrow went up "and I kind of freaked out. My roommate was a runner, and she convinced me to sign up for a half-marathon with her. Told me it would be a great way to get back in shape."

"Wait," he interrupted, "you had never ran before and you signed up for thirteen miles right out of the gate?"

"Thirteen point one," she said. "And there's a good chance alcohol was involved."

He laughed and asked, "How did it go?"

"I made it a whole half-mile that first day before I started puking."

"Oh no!"

"Oh yes, it was embarrassing. I decided that I was never going to run again. But my dad was pissed. He'd been proud of me when I signed up for the race and gladly bought me the best running shoes and anything else I needed. I wasn't allowed to back down now just because it had been a rough start."

"And you're still running now," he said.

"When I crossed that finish line, I was proud of myself. I had done exactly what I'd set out to do when I laced up those first running shoes. I had gotten myself back in shape and felt good not only physically, but mentally as well. Whenever I've a hit rough patch in my life, being able to get out for a run has helped me deal with it."

"That's a great story," he said. "Why did you think I would laugh at that?"

She shrugged. "I don't know. I guess because I was such a wuss about it in the beginning."

"But then you stuck with it in the end. That says something."

Jillian felt the familiar warmth in her cheeks as

she smiled.

"Thank you," she said softly.

Reid couldn't believe how well this was going. The conversation was flowing so naturally, and he loved watching her cute nose crinkle every time she laughed. But then the phone in his pocket vibrated. Reid glanced at it and remembered why dating was not a good idea in his line of work. He looked up and saw the concern in Jillian's face.

"Is everything all right?" she asked.

"It's work," he said, frowning. "I am so sorry, but I have to go."

CHAPTER THREE

"Now?" Jillian asked with confusion all over her face.

"Yes." He called the server over and handed her a credit card to pay for the meal. He didn't have time to wait for the check. He also wasn't going to have time to drive Jillian back to her house.

"Do you mind taking a cab home?" he asked.

Her jaw dropped.

"I only ask because I have to be there as soon as possible, and it would take me too long to drive to Renton and then back into Seattle."

She crossed her arms over her chest, and Reid immediately hated himself for putting her in this position.

"How about if you just drive my car home instead?" He couldn't believe he was offering to let someone else drive his Porsche, but he couldn't stand the idea of sending her off like this. "I'll take a cab into work and I can get a ride home when I'm done."

"No, it's fine," she said, standing up and grabbing her sweater off the back of the chair. Reid knew it was anything but fine.

"I don't mind taking a taxi home," she said and started walking to the front just as the server dropped the receipt for him to sign. Reid quickly scrawled his signature and took off after her. She was already asking the hostess to call a cab for her.

"I'm really sorry, Jillian," he said, following her out to the curb. "I told you I have to travel a lot. I just forgot to mention that it's usually last minute."

"I told you it's fine. I understand."

But she wouldn't look at him. Reid knew that this was the perfect out. He had already warned her that there was a reason he wasn't in a relationship. Now she would understand it firsthand and he could walk away. Future blowouts averted.

Instead, he kissed her. He didn't give any warning, just pulled her into him and pressed his lips against hers. He could feel her surprise at first, but then her whole body relaxed against his.

He slowly let her go just as a cab stopped in front of them. She was breathless, but also looking confused.

"I had hoped it would be on your doorstep," he said, "I'd had every intention of kissing you goodnight this evening."

He opened the door for her. She climbed in,

still staring at him without saying anything. Reid realized he had no idea if Jillian would ever speak to him again. Even if she had obviously enjoyed the kiss.

He leaned in and handed the driver more than enough to get her home.

"I'll call you when I get back," he said. "I promise."

When Reid walked in and discovered he had beat Aaron, he turned around to wait in his car, knowing Aaron would want an explanation. And almost slammed right into him.

"Jackson, what the hell are you doing here already?" he asked.

"I happened to be in the area," said Reid.

"Really? Doing what?" Aaron asked as they made their way to the briefing room. It was a simple enough question. Aaron was obviously just showing interest in his partner's personal life, but it was exactly the question Reid had been dreading. Yet he couldn't lie to the man who trusted him with his life.

"I was on a date," Reid said, keeping his eyes forward.

Before Aaron could respond, Rollins spotted them and motioned for them to sit so they could get started.

"If you will direct your attention to the screen," she said once they were seated, "you will see a Mode 5 cryptographer module, the transponders used for Identification Friend or Foe in military planes. You know about the two fighter planes that were shot down last week. When the wreckage was recovered, it was discovered that the modules were missing. Not a big concern, since they are useless without the key codes."

Rollins tapped the screen and a man's ID picture appeared.

"Yesterday this man, John Davies, went missing. He happens to be the Lead Cryptographer at Global Dynamic, the company that supplies the hardware and software for our IFF systems."

She tapped again and various surveillance photos popped up.

"One of our contacts spotted Davies in Mexico City with Trevor Melrone, a well-known middle man for hire. We don't know if Davies is there under duress, or if he has defected, but we need to get him out alive and keep those codes away from the transponder. Otherwise enemy aircraft will show up as friendly, and I don't need to explain the shit storm that will cause. Normally this would be the LA office's jurisdiction, but they're short-handed at the moment and requesting our assistance. The plane is on stand-by. As soon as you're ready, move out. Dismissed."

The cab pulled up in front of Jillian's house, and even though she knew Reid had given the driver more than enough to get her home, she still slipped the cabbie a couple extra dollars to tack onto the tip.

"Thanks," she muttered as she slid out.

She unlocked the door, her heart sinking even lower when she heard the news on the television, signaling her father was home. In the kitchen she found him popping a frozen meal into the microwave.

"Those will kill you, you know," she said, dropping her purse onto the counter.

"I thought you were out," he said.

"I was. But now I'm home." She hadn't told him it was a date and now she really didn't want to tell him how horribly it had ended. "Here, Papa, let me cook you something healthier. She pulled some chicken and veggies from the fridge.

"You don't have to," he said, but was already taking the uncooked meal out of the microwave.

"I want to. It's the least I can do for you letting me stay here until I can get back on my feet."

Jacob closed the freezer and gave her a kiss on the cheek. "*Tesoro*, you are always welcome in my home."

Jillian smiled at the Italian pet name. It was nice to know someone wanted her.

Yellow envelopes were waiting on their seats when Reid and Aaron boarded the plane about to take off for Mexico City. Reid opened his as soon as he sat down and found maps of the area around the hotel and dossiers on Trevor Melrone and John Davies, but Aaron simply laid his across his lap and continued to glare at Reid.

"So when you say date…" said Aaron.

"I mean a date with a girl," Reid said with a frown while continuing to look over the packet.

"The neighbor girl?"

"Yes."

"And how did that go?" asked Aaron.

Reid lowered the packet and finally looked at Aaron. "It was going just fine. Until I got the call to come in."

"How'd she react?"

Reid frowned again. "She wasn't too happy that I had to send her home in a cab."

Aaron started laughing and Reid regretted telling him.

"It was probably for the best," said Aaron.

"Yeah, whatever. Could we drop it now? We should be preparing for Mexico City."

Aaron opened his envelope and started to look over it. A couple of minutes later he shook his head and chuckled. "I can't believe you sent her home in a cab. Classy, man, real classy."

There was nothing Reid could do but try to ignore him.

With the *Wall Street Journal* in hand, Reid sat on the red velvet round in the middle of the expansive lobby of the Gran Hotel Ciudad de Mexico where Melrone had been sighted coming in and out of. Natural light streamed through the Tiffany stained glass roof from above, and even though Reid couldn't see him, he knew Aaron was somewhere on that fourth floor keeping an eye out for Melrone or Davies.

Reid turned another page in the newspaper.

"Target just walked in," Aaron said over the earpiece.

Reid made a casual glance around the lobby and spotted Melrone as well. "Got it."

Melrone strolled past Reid to the lift behind him, but Reid didn't move from his spot. After several minutes, Aaron's voice came over the earpiece again.

"He just got out on the third floor," he said. "Three doors down from the northeast corner. That means he's facing the square."

"I'm on it," said Reid. He folded up his newspaper and walked over to the reception desk.

"*¡Hola!*" said the dark-haired woman seated behind it.

"*¡Hola!*" he replied. "Do you speak English?" he asked.

"Of course," she said with a warm smile. "What can I do for you?"

Reid sat down. "I need to reserve a room. I was hoping for something facing the Constitution Square."

"Ah, the Zocalo," she said. "It is the most requested view."

"I realize that," he said. "It's just that my wife will be joining me later, and I thought that would be the most romantic."

She smiled at his gesture and started clicking away on her computer. "Let me see what I can do."

As she continued her search, Reid hoped this plan worked, because the other option was swiping a key and going in the front door. Because of the open halls over the lobby, that had too many variables.

"Well," she said, "I have one guest checking out and the room will be vacant for one night only before the next reservation arrives."

He smiled at her. "One night is all I need."

Darkness had fallen over the city as Reid stood on the balcony of the room watching the crowd in Constitution Square. A concert was playing on the opposite end, which he hoped would work in his favor rather than against. The fewer eyes in his direction, the better.

Reid checked his watch. "Another ten minutes and I'll just have to deal with Melrone."

"Copy that," said Aaron. "Hold up, Melrone just stepped out."

Reid picked up a coil of black rope.

"Following Melrone out of the building. It's now or never."

"Copy that," said Reid as climbed up onto the balcony and carefully but quickly crossed to the balcony three rooms over before fastening one end of the rope to the railing, letting the other end drop to the room below. He checked to make sure no one was paying attention before sliding down, balancing on the ledge just outside the room where Davies was thought to be.

"Where's Melrone?" Reid whispered.

"Still out," Aaron replied, "but he's just picking up food to go, so make it fast."

Reid pulled a blade and was about to jimmy the lock when he realized the window was already open a crack. He pushed on it and met no resistance. The curtains blew out into the cooler air, and Reid could see his target sitting in a chair facing the television with his back to him and no obvious restraints. Had Davies turned sides after all?

Making as little noise as possible, Reid climbed through the window and pulled out his sidearm.

"John Davies," Reid said quietly.

The man turned in his seat with a look of terror on his face. He raised his hands at the sight of Reid's gun.

"Who are you?" he asked.

Keeping his gun trained on Davies, Reid scanned the room to make sure there weren't any traps or sensors.

"You shouldn't be here," Davies said, panicking. "Why are you here?"

"Well, I believe I'm here to rescue you, Mr. Davies. Tell me what Melrone has on you. Why are you not walking out of this hotel right now?"

"They've threatened to kill my family," he said, trembling. "They showed me pictures of my son at school."

So the mission wasn't going to be quite that simple. Reid knew if they took Davies now without securing his family, Melrone would give the word as soon as he realized Davies was gone.

Aaron's voice came over the earpiece. "Melrone is headed back. You've got less than five minutes to get out of that room."

"Copy that." Reid turned back to Davies. "I'm going to make sure your family is out of harm's way and then we will get you out of here."

Davies nodded.

"Do you know why you were brought here?" Reid asked.

"Only that we are meeting someone tomorrow," Davies said, shaking his head. "But I don't know who. I'm guessing this has something to do with the transponders that were stolen last week. Am I right?"

"Yes."

"Melrone is in the hotel," said Aaron.

"I have to go," Reid told Davies. "But I'll be back once your family is safe. I just need you to hang in there."

Davies looked frightened, but nodded.

Reid climbed out the window and made his way back up the rope.

"Where's Davies?" Aaron asked when he stepped into the room only seconds after Reid.

"They've threatened his family," Reid told him. "We need to get to them first, but if we take his family before we grab Davies, he'll be that much harder to grab."

"Or they might just kill him," said Aaron.

"Or that." Reid grabbed the secure satellite phone. "This will have to be a coordinated effort."

It was just after two in the morning, and very few souls were moving about the hotel. Reid and Aaron stood outside Melrone's room, Reid with the satellite phone to his ear. On the other end was a tactical team ready to take Davies's family into custody.

Aaron knocked on the door a few times until Melrone finally opened it, half asleep. He never knew what hit him.

"Operation Jay Bird is a go," Reid said as he and Aaron walked into the room. "I repeat, Jay Bird is a go."

"Copy that," said the voice on the other end, and the line went dead.

Davies didn't need to be told what to do. He jumped from the bed and walked out of the room flanked by Reid and Aaron.

"A team is securing your family as we speak," Reid told Davies. "We need to get you to the extraction point. After a debriefing, you will be with them again."

"Thank you," he whispered.

The three of them took the elevator down to the ground floor where a single late check-in was happening at the same desk Reid had been sitting only twelve hours earlier.

Reid took a second glance at the desk and noticed three other men in close proximity. He'd be willing to bet money they were packing heat. The seated gentleman stood and turned in their direction, and Reid watched the impeccably dressed man do a double take of John Davies with confusion before looking to Reid. Anger began to swell in the man's face, and everything instantly clicked for Reid. This was the man Davies was supposed to be meeting tomorrow.

Reid pushed Davies down behind a couch just as the man reached into his jacket and pulled out a gun. A split second later his goons and Aaron were following suit, and the clerk at the desk was ducking for cover.

Reid fired off a shot before ducking behind the couch. A return shot sent a bullet right through the couch, narrowly missing him, and Reid knew it wasn't going to provide much cover.

"Get Davies out of here," shouted Aaron, "I'll cover you."

Reid stayed low as he pushed Davies towards the door while Aaron fired a quick succession of shots towards the four attackers. Reid and Davies stepped out onto the dark street that wasn't nearly as unpopulated as the hotel lobby had been. He made a quick assessment and realized the straightest line to the extraction point was through the Constitution

Square, but it also provided the least cover.

Aaron came rushing out. "Go, go, GO!"

Reid grabbed Davies' arm and pulled him as fast as the man would let him.

"If you want to see your family again, we need to run!" yelled Reid.

The shots continued to ring out, and Reid felt a bullet graze his arm as they were about to turn the only corner before the square.

Aaron stopped and turned to fire a couple more rounds, giving the other two a chance to get a few steps ahead.

When they crossed the street to the square, Reid was vaguely aware of a sharp pain in his lower back, but he didn't have time to think about it.

"Fuck this," Aaron said when he caught up to Reid. "We're never going to make it by foot."

"Agreed," said Reid as he turned to fire another shot, still keeping a tight grip on Davies.

On their side of the square, Reid saw a taxi unloading a fare and bee-lined it, knocking into the people waiting to get in. He shoved Davies into the back before turning to cover Aaron. The bystanders quickly got out of the way.

Aaron opened the front passenger side of the door and climbed in. "Drive!" he shouted to the flabbergasted driver.

Reid got in, but kept the door open just enough to aim a few more shots at the men chasing them, then closed it as they sped away. Reid twisted in his seat to look out the back window and saw two pissed men arrive where the taxi had been parked only moments ago.

"Fuck, Jackson," Aaron called from the front seat. "What happened to your back?"

Reid's hand reached around and felt the warm sticky liquid. He'd had his share of scrapes and bruises, but as Reid pulled his blood drenched hand back around, he didn't remember ever seeing this much red.

"I think I've been shot," he said quietly. As Reid's heart rate slowed, he could feel the pain replacing the adrenaline that had been coursing through his body.

"Davies," Aaron barked, "put your hand over it. We need to stop the bleeding."

All color had drained from Davies face, and he looked like he was trying to decide whether to puke or pass out.

"It's okay," said Reid. "I think I can put pressure on it from here." But his vision was already starting to blur.

"We're almost there," said Aaron. "Stay with me, Jackson!"

Aaron's voice sounded so far away. Reid could see Aaron's lips moving, but he couldn't make out the words as everything went black.

CHAPTER FOUR

Jillian walked into the back room during her break and pulled the phone from her locker. Still no word from Reid. Could it really be that hard for him to send a simple text? Maybe he was waiting for her to say something, she thought as she went into her messages. Maybe he was waiting to see how mad she was. Scowling, she shoved the phone back into her locker without sending anything. She *was* still mad. It was probably for the best that he wasn't calling her, she decided, and walked back out to her register.

Whispering. Soft, yet somehow grating whispers as Reid came to. He slowly opened his eyes, struggling to adjust to the brightness.

"He's very lucky," said a voice he didn't recognize. "Another inch north and he would've been looking at months of recovery, not days."

"So you're saying I won't have to train a new partner."

Reid smirked as he opened his eyes more fully. "You should be so lucky." The difficulty of the words surprised him.

Aaron and a doctor looked at Reid.

"Welcome back to the land of the living, Jackson," said Aaron. "You are one lucky son of a bitch."

"I don't feel lucky," Reid said, grimacing from the pain. "What the hell happened?"

"You were shot."

"But the vest…"

"The bastards had steel core bullets," said Aaron.

"Fuck," Reid muttered. "How bad is it?"

"Not as bad as you would expect," said the doctor. "Your vest may not have been able to stop it, but it was slowed considerably and settled into muscle without damaging any vital organs. The biggest concern was the blood loss. That's why you blacked out. We had to give you a transfusion before we could go in and attempt to remove the bullet. Your stitches can come out in about ten days and the muscle where you were shot is going to be tender for a while. But you should be good as new in no time."

"That's good to hear," said Reid scratching an itch on his left arm, but his fingernails only met with bandage. He looked at it, remembering the bullet graze, then to Aaron.

"How did you come out unscathed?" he asked.

"Guess I'm just more graceful," said Aaron.

Reid started to laugh, but was stopped short by the searing pain in his back.

Forty-eight hours later Reid was back at work, being debriefed with Aaron.

"This is the man who was supposed to meet with Davies?" Reid asked, looking up at the screen.

"Anton Casimir," said Rollins, "a for-profit terrorist. Born in the Ukraine, he was imprisoned at the age of sixteen for murdering his mother's abusive boyfriend. Two years later he escaped killing a guard in the process and has never stayed long in one place since. It is unclear if he was planning to use the codes and transponder directly or was selling them."

"Do we know where he is now?" asked Aaron.

Rollins shook her head. "We're not even sure if he's left Mexico yet, though I doubt he would have stuck around."

"Where does that leave us?" Reid wondered.

Rollins' expression soured. "As much as I hate to say this, there's nothing we can do but wait for him to resurface. But we kept the codes out of his hands, and the Davies family is safe again thanks to you gentlemen. I think we can still count this as a win."

Aaron and Reid nodded reluctantly.

"Now go finish up your mission logs. Dismissed."

Reid and Aaron were still doing paperwork when Rollins walked up and threw down a pair of tickets.

"Good job, men," she announced.

"What are these?" asked Aaron.

"Tickets to the Mariners' game tomorrow night against the Texas Rangers. You guys deserve a night out."

Reid shrugged and looked at Aaron.

"Should be fun," he said and Aaron nodded.

"Thanks, Director," said Aaron.

Rollins strode off and Aaron scribbled his signature at the bottom of the page and stood up.

"You want to meet me at the Pyramid Alehouse before the game?" he asked.

"Beer garden sounds good," said Reid.

"Are you still on the Vicodin?"

"Nah. It makes my head fuzzy. Maybe tonight, but just doing ibuprofen for now."

"You are one bad ass," said Aaron.

"Whatever. Four o'clock at the beer garden?"

"Four it is. Later, Jackson."

Aaron walked out and Reid finished up his own report. He grabbed his keys from the drawer and was headed out when Rollins caught up to him.

"Maxwell isn't going to be able to use his ticket," she said. "Do you know anyone who might want it?"

Reid was about to say no, but then thought of Jillian. He owed her big time.

"Sure, I know someone who might like it."

"Great." Rollins handed him the extra ticket and left Reid standing there wondering how Aaron was going to react when he brought her along.

The doorbell rang and when Jillian saw Reid through the peephole, she found herself with mixed emotions. After no word from him for three days, she was relieved to see he hadn't forgotten her completely. But she was still sore after being sent home halfway through their last date.

She did her best to appear blasé about his arrival before she opened the door. When she did, his face broke into a grin, and she felt her facade crumbling fast.

"Yes?" she asked.

Reid's smile faltered slightly at her icy tone.

"Hey," he said. "I just got home and wanted to apologize again for the other night."

Jillian crossed her arms. "Yes, you apologized the other night as well. You know, when you were pushing me into the cab."

His smile disappeared completely. As much as Jillian enjoyed seeing him squirm, she was a bit sad to see it go.

"I know. It was a disaster," he said, "but I was hoping to make it up to you." She raised a brow and he continued. "I have tickets to the baseball game tomorrow night and I was hoping you would come with me."

Inside, Jillian was jumping for joy that Reid was asking her out again. But a small part of her didn't know if it was such a good idea. The part that remembered the heartache of not so long ago.

"What do you say?" Reid asked when she hadn't responded.

"If I were to say yes," she said, and Reid's smile started to return, "should I drive my own car? You know, in case I need to find a ride home."

He frowned and Jillian had to admit it was almost as sexy as his smile.

"I deserve that," he said. "But I promise that I'm not on-call tomorrow. I'd be all yours. Although that is a rare thing," he added with caution in his voice, and Jillian understood completely. He was warning her, and she knew she had a decision to make.

"I suppose," she said slowly, and Reid's face lit up, "we could give it one more try."

"Great. I thought we'd go to the beer garden. It will take a while to find parking. Do you want to meet at my house at three?"

"I have to work until three," she said, shaking her head. "How about three-thirty so I can run home and change?"

"I can do three-thirty," he said. "See you tomorrow."

Jillian nodded and watched him walk back across the street before closing the door, hoping she wasn't making a big mistake. As eager as she was to get out there again, the truth was her heart was still very fragile.

Just after three there was a knock on the front door, and Reid opened it to find Jillian on his porch wearing a long causal cotton skirt and tank top with a sweater in her hand.

"Hello," he said.

"I was able to leave work a little early," she told him, smiling. "I knew you were hoping to head out sooner."

Reid grabbed his own jacket from a nearby closet. "I was all right with the later time, but this is great. You all ready then?"

She nodded.

"So where exactly did you have to take off to when we were at dinner?" Jillian asked as they pulled onto the freeway.

"New York," he replied with the ready answer.

"How long were you gone for?"

"The whole five days," he said. "I just got back yesterday morning. How was work today?" he asked in an effort to turn the conversation in a different direction.

She shrugged. "The usual. A lot of people that were going to the game as well. Or getting ready to watch it from home."

"I probably should have asked this before, but are you a baseball fan?"

"I can't stand baseball," she said.

Reid's head snapped in her direction and caught the playful grin on her face.

"I'm teasing," she said. "I don't normally follow baseball, but I always enjoy going to Safeco Field."

Reid turned his attention back to the road.

"You should have seen your face," she said, laughing. "Do you really think I would have agreed to come if I hated it so much?"

He couldn't help laughing with her. "I would hope not."

"Football is a different story though. I'm getting excited for the upcoming season."

"Have you been to any Seahawk games?"

"Loads," she said. "My dad has season tickets."

"I heard there was a waiting list for those."

"Now, but he's had his for years."

Reid noticed she didn't mention her mother and thought back to the pictures on her dresser.

"How about you?" she asked.

"I've been to a couple of games," he said. "I try to watch them if I'm home."

"Well, if my dad ever can't make it to a game, maybe I'll invite you."

Reid glanced over to catch her smile again. He liked it a lot better than the frown she was wearing at the end of their last attempt at a date. At least this time there wasn't any chance of him getting called in, so the odds were already improved.

Reid managed to find parking only a few blocks from the stadium, and they joined the throngs of people stepping off the buses nearby and migrating towards Safeco Field. Reid took Jillian's hand as they waited to cross an intersection, and she gave him a shy smile. His grip was sure and solid, and she couldn't help but imagine how those hands might feel…elsewhere. When the walk signal changed, he led her across the street to the Pyramid Alehouse beer garden where they waited to be carded before entering.

"I hope you don't mind," he said with a frown, "but I have a friend meeting us here."

"Oh." Jillian tried to hide her disappointment.

"The tickets were handed out at work so there will be other people in the stands I know, but Aaron and I made plans to meet here before the game."

She forced a smile. "That's fine."

They made it past the entrance and she scanned the crowd with Reid, not really knowing who they were looking for. But then she saw a man with chestnut-colored hair wave at them and Reid pulled her in that direction.

Maybe it was her imagination, but this man did not look happy to see her at all.

"Jillian," said Reid, "I'd like to introduce you to Aaron Wells. Wells, this is Jillian."

"Nice to meet you," Aaron said without any hint of a smile, but Jillian offered her hand nonetheless and he took it.

"Nice to meet you too," she said. "Reid just told me outside," she pointed over her shoulder, "that we would be meeting you."

"That's okay. He didn't tell me you would be here either." The two men exchanged a look.

"As I was headed out, the boss offered me an extra ticket. So I thought I would invite Jillian."

"Did you, now?" Aaron asked.

"Um, I'm going to go grab a beer," Jillian interrupted. "Can I get you anything?"

"I'll come with you," said Reid. "Be right back."

"I'll be waiting." Aaron said, taking a gulp of his own beer.

"What was that about?" Jillian asked while they waited in line.

"Sorry. Wells isn't exactly the warmest person. I had hoped he would be a bit more polite, but obviously I was asking too much."

"Is he going to be like this the whole time?" She frowned, envisioning an evening of Aaron's icy personality.

"Nah," said Reid. "I'm sure he'll warm up. Especially after a few beers."

"Can't wait," she muttered.

By the time the three of them found their seats at the ball field, Aaron's demeanor had not improved, despite the several beers he had downed. If Jillian hadn't been watching him drink them, she would have guessed him stone-cold sober. Or at least stone-cold. Reid was trying his best to pull them into joined conversation, even brought up football, but Aaron just shrugged or grunted his answers.

The second inning had just started when Reid, who had been sitting between them, left to go to the bathroom. She and Aaron sat in silence watching the game, which was even slower than usual, when Jillian couldn't take it any longer.

"Did I do something to you?" she asked, looking right at him. He was leaning forward with an elbow on his knee and chin in his hand.

"No. Why?" he asked, still staring straight ahead.

"So you're just always this rude."

He ran his thumb along his square jaw. "Yep."

"How did you and Reid ever become friends?"

Aaron sat up and put an arm over the back of Reid's empty chair.

"Oh, I'm not this rude to my friends," he said, watching the second baseman catch a grounder.

Jillian's jaw dropped. "What the hell did I do to piss you off like this?"

He finally looked at her. "Listen, it's nothing personal. I just know that whatever is going on between you and Reid will never work. So I don't see any point in trying to get chummy with you. You seem like a nice girl, in all honesty. But if you haven't noticed yet that Reid's job isn't exactly conducive to dating, you will soon enough."

"Don't you think you should let me and perhaps Reid be the judge of that?"

Aaron shrugged.

"I need a beer," she said, standing up. Jillian could not bear to be around this man a second longer.

Reid passed her in the aisle.

"Where you going?" he asked.

"I need a beer," she said a little louder this time and stomped down the stairs to the nearest concession stand and got in line. God, she was tired of lines.

Someone stepped in behind her and she didn't think anything of it, until she heard the whisper in her ear.

"Do you miss me yet?"

She spun around, hoping it was her imagination.

"Cameron," she seethed, coming face to face with her ex-boyfriend.

CHAPTER FIVE

Reid sat back down in his seat, unable to shake the feeling Jillian was upset. Did he do or say something wrong? He glanced over at Wells, who happened to be looking very smug.

"What did you do?" Reid asked.

"What are you talking about?"

"You know what I'm talking about. Why did Jillian just stomp off?"

"Why did you bring her, Jackson?"

"I told you. Rollins gave me an extra ticket. I figured I owed her after the shitty date last time."

"That shitty date was a perfect example of why you two shouldn't be dating."

"What the hell did you say to her?" Reid asked.

"I told her that you two were never going to work."

"Christ, Wells. Couldn't you just leave your mouth shut for one day?" Reid got up and went to find Jillian.

"You're welcome," Aaron shouted.

"How's it going, Jillian?" Cameron asked.

"What the hell are you doing here?" God she wanted to wipe that smug look off his face.

"Thousands of people are here." Cameron waved his hand around the stadium. "Why shouldn't I be one of them?"

She turned back around to the line that wasn't making much progress.

"So what have you been up to lately?" Cameron wasn't taking the hint.

"Not much, seeing as how nobody will hire me." She rounded on him again. "But you already knew that."

Cameron frowned, but he couldn't hide the amusement in his eyes. "Pity. You could always come work for me again."

Jillian slapped him, surprising herself.

"Damn, Jillian." His hand went to the reddening cheek. "I never knew you had it in you. Maybe if you'd shown this kind of passion in the bedroom, I wouldn't have slept with Tina."

Maybe it was all the pent up anger. Maybe it was her recent interaction with Aaron. Perhaps she'd even had too many beers. Jillian started wailing on Cameron.

"You…little…piece…of…shit," she said between punches. Everything else around her blurred, and she ignored his yells for her to stop.

Then someone's arms were around her, pulling her off of Cameron.

"Let me go!" she screamed, straining against whoever was trying to stop her. "The asshole deserves it."

"Jillian!"

She stopped, realizing it was Reid who was holding her. She tried to catch her breath before facing him and saw the crowd that had gathered around them and security not far off running in their direction.

Cameron's face peeked out from behind his arms. "Jeez, Jillian. What the fuck was that for?"

Jillian tried to lunge for him again, but Reid tightened his grip on her.

"What's going on here?" said the yellow-jacketed gentleman.

"I'll tell you what happened," said Cameron, "this bitch attacked me for no reason."

She sucked in a breath and felt Reid prepare for her to pull away again, but she resisted the urge this time.

"Ma'am, is this true?"

"I wouldn't say for no reason. This man is my ex," she could hear Reid gasp from behind her, "and the reason I can't find a job anymore."

Cameron said nothing, but she could see the twisted amusement in his eyes again.

"Be that as it may," said the security guard, "you can't attack people. I'm afraid I'm going to have to ask you to leave."

"What?"

Reid's arms finally released her. "Sir, is that really necessary?" he said.

The gentleman nodded. "We have a zero tolerance policy on fighting."

"But what about him?" Jillian asked, gesturing to Cameron.

"Was he hitting you as well?"

"Well, no."

He shrugged. Unbelievable. First Cameron cost her her job, and now he was getting her kicked out of the ball park. And life continued to go on as usual for him.

"Ma'am." He gestured towards the exit.

"Can I at least grab my stuff?" she asked.

"Yes. I'll escort you."

Reid said nothing, but followed them both back up to the seat. How embarrassing. Their second date was being cut short, and this time it was entirely her fault. *It must be a sign.*

Aaron shot a glance at Jillian as she made her way down the row and did a double take, noticing the guy in the big yellow jacket following her.

"What's going on, Jackson?" It only added to her irritation that he was not addressing her.

"I'm afraid Jillian and I are going to have to duck out early," said Reid.

"You don't have to leave because of me." Jillian muttered, picking up her bag and sweater. "I'm sure I can catch a cab home. Again."

Reid caught her arm when she stepped back into the aisle.

"I'm not letting you take a taxi home."

She looked over her shoulder at Aaron. "What about Mr. Sunshine over there?"

Reid smiled at her jab. "I'm sure he'll be fine. I'll call you later, Wells."

Aaron looked confused, and then pissed, as he waved good-bye. Jillian didn't really care.

Security walked the two of them to the nearest exit and confiscated their tickets before sending them on their way.

Reid kept step with Jillian, who was walking with her arms crossed and eyes focused on the sidewalk.

"You didn't have to leave," she said without looking up.

"I wasn't going to stay without you."

They walked another block in silence before Reid asked, "Are you going to tell me what that was all about? Or should I worry about being attacked on random outings."

She looked at him in shock and he smiled. "I was only joking. I don't really think you're going to attack me." Reid put an arm around her. "Plus, unlike that poor loser back there, I think I could take you."

Jillian tried to hide it, but Reid caught the hint of a smile on her face. "C'mon, let's get you home," he said.

He opened the passenger door for her, and she paused before climbing in.

"Do you think this is a sign?"

He frowned. "What do you mean?"

"Date number one, you had to…leave early. And now on date number two I managed to get us kicked out of Safeco Field. Do you think it's a sign?"

"I don't believe in signs. I'm assuming you don't make it a habit to get kicked out of ball games."

"That was a definitely a first for me," she said.

"And while I often have to leave at a moment's notice, it's because of the nature of my work, nothing personal."

"So you'd be open to going out with me again?"

"Who says tonight is over already? Hop in. I have an idea."

Her forehead wrinkled, but she climbed in.

"Are you going to tell me what this idea is?" she asked as he turned onto the freeway.

"Are you going to tell me what the fight was about?"

"Do I have to?"

"No, of course not," he said. "But would you be interested in going on a motorcycle ride with me?"

"A motorcycle," she whispered.

"Yes. Have you ever ridden one?"

She shook her head.

"Would you like to?"

"Is it safe?" she asked.

"With me, it is"

"Okay."

"So now are you going to tell me your story?"

Jillian sighed. "He's my ex-boyfriend."

"I heard you tell the security guard. And how did he cost you your job?"

"Well," she said slowly, "he was my boss."

"You were dating your boss?"

"He didn't start out as my boss. We worked for the same company, just not together. Eventually he ended up in that position."

"What happened? Did you guys break up and he fired you?"

"No, I quit."

"You quit? I don't understand."

"I found out he was cheating on me with his assistant, so I moved out and quit my job. All in the same week."

Reid didn't blame Jillian one bit for going ape shit on the guy.

"But I'm still not sure I follow how that cost you your job if you're the one that quit."

"He won't give me a decent reference. I keep applying for other jobs in my field, but that position was the only one I'd had and without it on my resume, I'm having trouble getting an interview. But when they do the reference check, Cameron tells them that I was a lazy employee or something. And that is why even though I have a very expensive degree in graphic design, I am working as a cashier at Safeway and living with my dad."

"You should be talking to *his* supervisors. Let them know what he is doing."

"Problem is his father owns the company. I've thought about suing, but I think it would be more trouble than it's worth. I'll figure it out eventually. I'm sure he'll tire of this game."

She turned to stare out the window, and Reid noticed her slumped shoulders, as though she were admitting defeat.

"Hey," he said, and she turned back around. "I think you showed him today that he's been messing with the wrong woman."

She smiled. "Thanks. But just so you know, I don't usually attack ex-boyfriends, or anyone for that matter. I guess I was caught off guard running into him like that. And especially after—"

"After what?" he asked.

"Nothing, never mind."

"No, what were you going to say? After what?"

"Right before I had gone downstairs, Aaron and I were arguing. That's to say that I was already in an irritated mood when I ran into Cameron."

"Aaron told me he talked to you. Sorry about that. Don't mind him."

She started to say something, but they were

pulling up in front of her dad's house.

"It's going to be chilly on the bike," he said, stopping the car. "Why don't you change into jeans, grab a warmer jacket, and meet me in my garage?"

She nodded and climbed out. Reid watched her walk into the house before pulling into his driveway.

As Jillian walked up to Reid's house, he was rolling out a red motorcycle. Even she, who knew nothing about bikes, could appreciate the beauty of this machine. She had a feeling this was going to be fun.

"What kind of motorcycle is this?" she asked.

"A Ducati 1199 Panigale," he said with such reverence that Jillian couldn't help but smile. "Grab the two helmets off the shelf," he instructed, pointing to the right side of the garage.

"The rules are simple enough," Reid said when she had brought them over. "Lean into the turns with me. You don't need to put your feet down when we stop. That's my job."

Jillian nodded, trying to soak it all in.

"Experienced passengers," he continued, "will often just place their hands on their knees while riding."

He stepped closer and placed a hand on one of the helmets she was holding.

"But you can hold onto me as tight as you need to feel safe," he said quietly and Jillian felt a tingle sweep though her whole body. "I promise you won't fall off the back. You're safe with me. Got it?"

She nodded again.

"Good. Now let's get this helmet on you." He took the helmet from her hand and helped her put it on, tucking her hair into it.

"When we're stopped," he said, "you can put the visor up to talk, but once we get going, you'll want it down to protect you from the wind. Not to mention the bugs."

She made a face and he laughed. *Oh, I'm in trouble.*

"How fast will we be going?" she asked.

"As fast as you want," he answered.

There was no stopping the childish grin on her face. Her father would *kill* her if he knew what she was about to do.

Reid helped her on the bike before sliding on in front of her. Jillian had always thought of motorcycles as small, because she was comparing them to the other vehicles on the road. But now that she was straddling it, the bike felt massive between her legs. Reid started the engine and Jillian's adrenaline surged as it roared to life beneath her.

She wrapped her arms around his midsection. He felt solid against her. She inhaled him, and this time was able to get a good breath of his intoxicating scent. Musky, with just a hint of citrus.

Reid slowly made his way to the main road and waited for oncoming traffic to clear before turning up the hill where he shot off, quickly reaching the speed limit. Jillian squeezed harder and felt him chuckle at her reaction.

He had to stop at the top of the hill for a red light and threw up his visor.

"Any idea where you want to go?" he shouted over his shoulder.

Jillian shook her head. "Surprise me," she yelled back. She just caught his grin before he slammed the visor back down and accelerated with the green light.

Reid headed east along Petrovitsky Road that went from four lanes down to two, and the turns were just enough to be fun, but not too dangerous. As he picked up speed, Jillian could hear nothing but wind and the bike's engine. It was white noise as she closed her eyes, shutting out everything but the exhilaration coursing through her. Another tingle, a shiver really, swept over her, and Jillian wasn't entirely sure if it was caused by the cool air whipping around them, or the man she currently had her arms wrapped around— whom she admittedly knew very little about.

It's the wind, she told herself. I*t's just the* *wind.*

The bike slowed as Reid came to the end of Petrovitsky, but a couple more turns and they were racing onto a highway that would take them even further from home, towards the Cascade Mountains. This time Jillian opened her eyes to watch everything go rushing by. She sneaked a look over Reid's shoulder and saw the illuminated display reading a speed of almost a hundred miles per hour. This was dangerous. It had to be. But she was loving every second of it. Jillian had no idea where they were going, and she didn't care.

At the high speed, it wasn't long before they were pulling up to Snoqualmie Falls, just as the sun was preparing to call it a day.

Reid killed the engine and let Jillian climb off before he put the kickstand down. They removed their helmets and placed them on the bike.

"How was it?" he asked as they walked over to the covered observation deck near the base of the two hundred sixty-eight foot waterfall.

"Incredible," she said. Her smile was contagious, and Reid found himself grinning as well.

At the lookout, they leaned against the railing facing the water. The dry summer meant the falls weren't at their most powerful, but that made for easier conversation. The hotel next to the top of the falls caught Reid's attention.

"Have you ever stayed at The Salish Lodge?" he asked.

"No," she answered. "I've had breakfast there a couple of times. It's pretty good." She paused. "My parents would always book a room for their anniversary."

Again Reid thought of the pictures on her dresser.

"You never mention your mom," he said

slowly.

"She passed away when I was fourteen. Ovarian cancer."

"Fourteen? That must have been a rough age for a girl to lose her mother."

"Is there ever an age when it isn't rough?" she asked.

Reid frowned. "Not really, I guess."

"It was pretty hard on my dad as well. Shortly after the funeral I was sent to stay with my aunt for a month. I still don't know if it was his idea or my aunt's, but I think it was pretty clear to everyone that he wasn't in any shape to take care of me. And then shortly after I went home, he started taking me to the gun range and teaching me how to shoot. It was so random. I think it made him feel he could protect me better or something."

Reid didn't know what to say, so he just wrapped an arm around her. Jillian stood there, letting him comfort her, but then she suddenly moved herself out of his reach and turned her back to the falls.

"That was a long time ago though," she said. "Enough about me. I feel like I'm always doing all the talking. Tell me something about you."

"Well, I've never been kicked out of a ball game before," he said, causing Jillian to blush. He loved that he could bring the color to her cheeks so easily.

"I'm so sorry," she said.

"Seriously, don't worry about it." He took a

step in her direction. "If it had really bothered me, I wouldn't have left with you, and I certainly wouldn't be here with you now." The color in her cheeks deepened, and Reid pushed back a hair that was sticking to her cheek.

"What about your family?" she asked, changing the subject. But she hadn't moved away from him this time. "Do you get out east to see them often?"

Reid sighed and turned his back to the falls as well.

"My story isn't much better. My parents were killed in a car accident when I was in high school. I was in a group home for a year until I was able to get emancipated. Just barely made it into MIT, got a job with Alliance Security Systems, and now here I am."

"You didn't have any other family?" she asked.

"Nope."

"How sad."

Reid shrugged. "I survived."

He glanced at the orange sky, quickly turning gray. "It's getting late. I should get you home."

She nodded and they walked back.

"You ready for round two?" Reid asked as they put their helmets back on, and there was the grin that made his heart stop.

"Absolutely," she said.

Night had completely fallen by the time they

were pulling in to Reid's garage. He shut off the engine and they climbed off the bike. Jillian removed her helmet and handed it to Reid as she ran her fingers through her hair.

Thank you," she said. "That was exactly what I needed."

"My pleasure," he said, placing the helmets back on the shelf.

"So, um, how long have been riding motorcycles?" she asked.

Reid sensed she wasn't ready to go home, which was okay with him. He wasn't ready for her to leave either.

"A while now." He moved closer to where she was still standing by the bike. "If you ever want to go again," another step closer, "just let me know."

Jillian remained rooted to her spot, but the increase in her breathing was obvious to Reid. He was so close now. All he'd have to do is reach out to touch her. The thought of his hands on her skin made his own pulse quicken. His mind began picturing her naked on his bed upstairs.

"It's getting late," she said suddenly. "I bet you're wanting to get to bed."

The corner of his mouth went up. She had no idea.

"I don't mind the company," he said. "Unless you're wanting to get home?"

"No," she whispered.

It was the invitation Reid was looking for. He

reached out to pull Jillian into him and his mouth was immediately on hers. This time there was no surprise, no hesitation as she kissed him back. He slowly unzipped her jacket and moved his palms underneath it to her back. Jillian's body pressed harder against his and Reid cupped her bottom, lifting her off the floor. Their lips stayed locked as he carried her the short distance to the workbench and dropped her on the flat surface. She giggled and went to work on Reid's jacket. He let it fall to the floor before sliding Jillian's off. His mouth worked its way to her ear and then down her throat while a hand moved under her shirt, feeling the warm flesh against it.

"What about the neighbors?" she said breathlessly.

"What about them?" Reid murmured into her neck. The shirt inched higher.

"The door is still open."

Reid looked out at the quiet street. "Oh, that."

Without any warning, he threw Jillian—who giggled again—over his shoulder, and carried her into the kitchen, making sure to hit the garage door button on the way out.

The granite was hard beneath Jillian as Reid set her down on the kitchen island, but she didn't mind. All she cared about right now was Reid's strong and very capable hands on her hot skin. She pulled her shirt off, giving him easier access. His lips grazed her breast just above the bra, and she arched back where

Reid's arms were ready to support her.

He was kissing her lips again, and Jillian's tongue welcomed him. If only she never had to breathe again.

Then Reid was pushing her farther along the counter, and one knee at a time, climbed up onto it. Jillian had to lay back as Reid worked his way on top of her. He sat up and straddled her for a second to remove his own shirt, and then hovered over her again.

She ran her fingers through his hair before pulling his face into hers. He just tasted too damn good.

Reid's hand slid roughly down her torso to the top of her jeans and undid the button. And then the zipper.

Jillian whimpered as Reid traced a finger along the top of her underwear. But just as she thought he was about to go further, the finger started moving north and slipped under her bra, circling the nipple. Soon the whole breast was freed of its confines and Reid's tongue gently licked it. Her chest rose, forcing it harder against his mouth. Again, just as Jillian thought he would keep going, Reid was slipping the bra back on, and his mouth migrated to her neck and nipped at her ear. She groaned and dug her nails into his chest in frustration.

Reid chuckled. "Is this too much for you?" he breathed into her ear.

"You really know how to drive a girl crazy,"

she said.

"I'm only," he kissed a shoulder, "getting," the curvature of her neck, "started."

He looked down at her and Jillian stared back at his seductive grin. It was a beautiful face, so strong and confident. Just the kind of thing to break a girl's heart.

She started to shake her head and Reid's smile faded.

"What is it?" he asked.

"I'm sorry," she said. "I'm so *so* sorry. I can't."

Reid climbed down off the counter, looking thoroughly confused. Jillian felt horrible, but she knew she would just feel worse in the morning.

"I should go." She jumped down and threw on her shirt. She looked down the hall to the front door and bolted for it.

The next morning Reid was knocking on Jillian's front door. He'd found her jacket in the garage and had debated whether to take it over or wait until she came back for it. He still didn't understand what went wrong the night before.

The door opened and Reid was disappointed to find Jacob, not Jillian on the other side of it.

"Mr. Sandro?" Reid asked.

"Yes?"

"I'm Reid Jackson. I live just across the street," he said, pointing to his house.

"You're the one who helped Jillian when she hurt her ankle."

"I did," said Reid. "I'm sorry to bother you, but Jillian left her jacket at my house last night and I just wanted to return it."

Jacob's forehead creased. "She was with you last night?"

"Yes, sir." Reid wondered what Jillian had told her father.

"Do you know where she is now?" Jacob asked.

"I'm sorry? I thought she was here."

The color drained from Jacob's face. "She never came home last night."

CHAPTER SIX

The first thing Jillian noticed was an insane pounding in her head and something cold and hard pressing against her right cheek. The next was talking in another room. She slowly opened her eyes, but it didn't help much. Very little light was coming into wherever she was. She tried to focus on the glow in front of her and realized it was the bottom of a door. Jillian attempted to push up off what she now assumed to be a concrete floor, but it was too much for her. Laying in the dark room, she tried to remember what had happened. How did she get here? She had left Reid's house and was almost to her door when…When what? The pain in her head suggested someone had hit her hard. But why did she feel so groggy now? Did somebody drug her? Panic started to creep in. Someone had kidnapped her. And she was still alive, so they clearly weren't done with her.

"Oh, God," she groaned as every bad scenario possible ran through her mind. In an effort to keep from losing it completely, she concentrated on the voices outside the door, hoping to learn something. But they were mostly muffled, and what she could pick up didn't sound anything like English.

There was a commotion outside, someone barking orders, and then the door was opened and Jillian blinked against the bright light now spilling in. A large man walked in and scooped her up. The larger room he carried her into suggested a warehouse. There were four other men besides the one carrying Jillian, most of them in black with guns slung across their chests. But one man was dressed in a tailored gray suit that matched his eyes, and if he had a gun on him, it was hidden. She was set on a hard chair and the gray suit moved towards her.

"*Otrymaty ïy˘vody,*" he snapped.

Someone brought him a glass of water and he kneeled in front of her. He lifted the glass to her lips, and Jillian drank from it with his help. She hadn't realized how parched her mouth was and took the glasses with both hands, finishing it without assistance.

"Better, Miss Sandro?" the gray suit asked in a thick accent and she nodded.

"How do you know my name?" she asked. "What do you want with me?"

"All in due time. Come. We are going for a little ride."

[77]

Someone helped Jillian to her feet. She was still unsteady, but could feel the strength slowly returning to her body.

A silver Mercedes was parked outside, and she and the gray suit climbed in the back with two of the armed men in front while the other two got into a dark SUV. A simple black cell phone lay on the back seat and Jillian looked at it questioningly.

"I am expecting a call from a mutual acquaintance of ours any minute now," said her abductor.

Jillian couldn't fathom who they possibly had in common.

"What do you mean she never came home last night?" Reid asked Jacob. "She left my place around ten last night."

Jacob shook his head. "I stayed up until midnight, but she never came home. I've been trying to call her cell phone, but she's not answering."

This didn't make sense to Reid. He saw her walk out the front door. She'd had no wallet, so it wasn't likely she would have gone anywhere else but home. So then what happened in the fifty feet from his house to hers?

"I'm sure there's a reasonable explanation, Mr. Sandro. But I'll see what I can find out and you let me know if you hear from her."

Jacob nodded, but didn't look convinced.

"Don't worry," said Reid. "I'm sure she's

safe."

As Reid walked back to his house, he pulled out his phone and dialed Aaron.

"If you're calling to apologize—" Aaron started, but Reid cut him off.

"She's gone missing, Wells."

"What do you mean missing? How do you misplace a whole woman?"

"She left my house last night and apparently never made it home."

"Maybe you scared her off," said Aaron, but Reid was only half listening. Something sitting on the front porch caught his attention.

"If you ask me," continued Aaron, "it's for the best."

"Shut up, Wells. I'm going to have to call you back." Reid hung up on his protests and collected the cell phone sitting on his mat. He looked around. This hadn't been sitting here when he left the house just minutes ago.

Reid walked into the house, examining the phone. It was very basic, most likely a burner. He checked the contacts and found a single number saved. Reid dialed it. After the fourth ring it picked up, but there was only silence on the other end.

"Hello," he said.

"Reid?" said a quiet voice.

"Jillian?"

"Reid! What's going—" She was cut off.

"Jillian!"

"Hello, Agent Jackson." The new voice was heavily accented. Reid recognized it as Russian. No. Ukrainian.

"Who the hell is this?" Reid asked.

"I still need those codes, Mr. Jackson."

"Casimir?"

"Very good," said Casimir.

"I don't have those codes."

"If you ever want to see your lovely friend again," Casimir told him, "you will get them."

Reid was as confused as ever. How the hell did Casimir even know to go after Jillian?

"Even if I could get them," said Reid, "what makes you think I would hand them over for her? She's just my neighbor."

"We both know that she is more to you than just a neighbor. But, if that is how you feel… Shall I put a bullet in her brain now?" Reid heard a gasp from Jillian in the background and closed his eyes. "Or would you like to put her father on the phone first, so that he can say good-bye to his only daughter? Isn't losing his wife to cancer bad enough?"

Reid's eyes flew open as he remembered the night Jillian asked him over.

"Jillian wasn't being paranoid last week, was she?" he asked. "You were in her house."

Casimir laughed. "Well, not me personally. But yes, I have been watching her. She really is quite lovely when she sleeps."

Reid's stomach turned. "But how did you

know she was even connected to me? I'd only just met her at that point." His head was swimming with all the questions.

"That is not something you should worry about right now. You need to figure out how you are going to get those codes to me."

Reid knew that was never going to happen, but admitting it would only get Jillian killed. He needed to buy her time.

"Put her on the phone," he said.

"We have a deal, no?" asked Casimir.

"Just put her on the damn phone," Reid growled.

"Reid?" Jillian's voice was shaking.

"Have they hurt you?" he asked.

"No. Well, yes, but—Reid, what the hell is going on?"

"I need you to listen to this man, Jillian. His name is Anton Casimir and he is incredibly dangerous," he said. "But I will come for you. I just need you to be strong. Can you do that for me?"

"Yes," she said, and Reid believed her. Now he just needed to hold up his end of the deal.

"Good. Put Casimir back on the phone. I'll see you soon."

"Okay."

Casimir's voice came on the line again. "You have very good taste, Agent Jackson. It would be a shame for her to become—what is the words— collateral damage. A waste even."

"If you lay a finger on her I'll—"

"You will what?" Casimir laughed. "You are in no position to make threats."

Reid took a deep breath. "What's the plan?"

"Good. We are on same page then. I think the best solution is for you to bring me John Davies."

"He's in protective custody," said Reid. "Even I can't touch him."

"The how, Agent Jackson, is not my problem. If you ever want to see these beautiful brown eyes again, you will bring him, or something just as valuable, to me. You have twenty-four hours, when I will call with further instruction. Keep this phone on you, Agent Jackson. And don't do anything stupid."

The line went dead.

Anton Casimir pocketed the phone and exited the Mercedes.

"Come, Miss Sandro," he said, extending a hand to help her out.

Jillian considered her captor holding the door open as she slid out without taking his hand. She always imagined kidnappers to be hard ruthless men. Thugs even. Yet this man struck her as well-groomed and polished. His salt-and-pepper hair was cleanly cut and brushed forward with a straight cut over the bangs. The severe scar over his left eye was the only thing suggesting he had ever been involved in any kind of scuffle. That and his threatening gaze. She looked out to the end of the pier they had just arrived at. She also never imagined them owning such impressive yachts.

They stepped onto the aft end of a ship with an outdoor seating area, complete with lounge chairs and a small hot tub. Casimir led her past this through sliding doors and into a plush living room decorated in rich wood and stark white. Beyond this room was a dining area, where breakfast items had been laid out and a gentleman in dress slacks and a button-down shirt was seated, typing something into his phone. He looked up and flashed a smile that Jillian felt was far too charming given the situation.

"Is this her?" he asked in a British accent as he stood.

Casimir nodded and walked up to the table to sample a custard.

"*Dobre,*" he said, nodding.

A steward Jillian hadn't even noticed in the corner nodded and left the room.

"This had better work," said the English stranger.

Casimir waved him off. "It is all going according to plan."

The English stranger stepped into Casimir's space. Jillian could see the annoyance in Casimir's face, but he said nothing as the blue-eyed gentleman spoke.

"That's what you told me last time. You'd better be right, because I won't be cleaning up your fucking mess again."

The corner of Casimir's mouth twitched into a slight sneer. The other man put his hands into his pockets and strode off towards the door.

"Now, if you don't mind," he said, "I promised to take my Love to brunch this morning." He was almost out the door when he turned to Jillian and said, "Good luck to you, Miss Sandro. I hope for both our sakes that Reid Jackson is up to the task." And he was gone.

"Sit," Casimir instructed Jillian. "We will eat."

"I'm not hungry," she said quietly.

"It was not a question."

"Being hit, drugged, and kidnapped kind of killed my appetite," she said. "I'm not hungry.

Casimir's stone gray eyes burned into her, but she stood her ground, until he slapped her across the face with the back of his hand so hard that she fell to the ground.

"I told you it was not a question," he said, adjusting the cuff of his right sleeve. "Now get up before you drip blood on the carpet."

Jillian touched her stinging lip. The ring on his finger had split it. She stood up and sat down on the chair, fighting back tears.

"Good," said Casimir as he took his seat. "Was that so hard?"

Reid had tried to warn her how dangerous he was. Which again begged the question, how did Reid know this man?

"Eat," Casimir ordered and this time Jillian

knew better.

Her unsteady hand speared a piece of cantaloupe from her plate and she forced it to her mouth. It was ripe and juicy, but all Jillian could taste was the metallic tang of her own blood.

Reid pocketed the burner phone and redialed Aaron.

"Casimir has Jillian," he said the second Aaron picked up.

"That's insane. What would Casimir want with Jillian?"

"He's offering to trade her for John Davies," said Reid. "Or the codes. Neither of which I have access to."

"This still doesn't make any sense. How would he even know about her?"

"I haven't figured that part out yet."

"You need to go to Rollins," Aaron told him.

"I can't," said Reid. "She'd be dead before they figured out what to do. And chances are they would decide to do nothing. We don't negotiate with terrorists, remember?"

"Jesus, Jackson. You're looking at treason just for thinking about giving Casimir what he wants."

"I'm not an idiot," said Reid. "Of course I'm not going to give him anything."

"That what are you going to do?"

"I have to get Jillian."

It was so quiet on the other end that Reid

thought the call had been dropped until Aaron let out a long, slow breath.

"I'll help you," he said.

"I can't let you risk everything too."

"And what the hell am I supposed to do? Just sit here on my hands and hope everything works out for you? Not happening, man."

"Be my support then," said Reid. "Help me get info when I need it."

"I can do that. What's your first move?"

Now the silence came from Reid's end.

"Jackson?"

"I'm thinking." Reid remembered his conversation with Casimir. "He told me not to do anything stupid, which means he probably has someone tailing me." He wondered if someone was watching him now. Whoever dropped the phone couldn't be far. They might even be listening to him right this minute.

"I'm headed to Sea-Tac," he said into the phone. "I think I might know where Davies is."

"But I thought—"

Reid cut him off. "I'll call you when I have more info."

CHAPTER SEVEN

The Seattle-Tacoma International airport was packed as usual with travelers as Reid got in line for the nearest ticketing agent. He scanned the crowd, looking for anyone suspicious and found him almost immediately, but kept looking. In a terminal full of business travelers and flustered families, the man in a fedora stood out like a sore thumb. He had no luggage and wasn't standing in any of the lines, just leaning against a trash and can smacking his gum. Casimir wanted Reid to know that he was being watched, perhaps to keep Reid from veering off course. All that meant was that Reid had to be at least two steps ahead.

Reid walked up to the counter.

"Hello," he said to the smiling agent behind the computer. "I need a ticket for the first flight you have available to Washington D.C."

Her smile faded as she typed away at the keyboard.

"I have a flight that leaves later this morning, but it has a layover in Atlanta and you won't land in DC until ten o'clock eastern time tonight."

Reid glanced over his shoulder in the direction of the man watching him. He just had to go through the motions. If Casimir thought he was on a plane all day, that gave him several hours to get a plan in motion.

"That will be perfect," he said.

"Great, I just need identification and a credit card."

Reid pulled out his wallet.

"And will you be checking any luggage?" she asked, taking the cards from him.

"Nope, I'm good"

Reid waited for her to print off his tickets and then walked over to security. His companion followed him only as far as another nearby garbage can to lean against. This was perfect. Reid made it through security and disappeared around a corner. He peeked back around just in time to see the man pull out a cell phone as he started to walk away.

Reid rushed to an exit point and made his way towards the nearest skybridge leading to the parking garage, when he saw a man in a white fedora exiting the double doors at the opposite end. Reid raced across the vestibule and came out in time to see him step onto an elevator. Since it was only ground transportation on the lower levels, Reid hit the up button and watched the LED screen above the elevator Mr. Fedora had stepped on. Every time another set of doors opened, Reid pushed the up button again, ignoring the confused stares from other patrons. He had to know where *this* elevator was headed. Reid lucked out; it made one stop only on the fifth level before heading back down. Now he jumped into the first open elevator and took it up two floors. He ran along the aisles, trying to keep his head low, until he caught sight of his man in the far north corner and Reid hurried over before his opportunity was gone. The man climbed into his car. Reid hid behind a pole. All he needed was a license number. Creeping between two vehicles, he pulled out his phone and snapped a picture of the plates as the driver backed out. Reid dropped to the ground and rolled under an Acura as Mr. Fedora swung out wide to straighten his wheels before driving off.

Reid rolled back out and called Aaron while making his way back to his own car.

"Jackson, where are you at?"

"About to leave Sea-Tac. I was being followed, but I just lost him. I'm sending you a picture of his license plate. I need you to get me a name and address and then meet me at my place."

"That's easy enough. See you soon."

Reid started his car and put it into reverse, but then immediately slammed it into park again. He climbed out and started feeling along the undercarriage until he found what he was looking for. A tracker had been placed under the passenger side door. After a quick glance to make sure no one was watching, Reid climbed onto the running board of his car and stuck the magnetic tracker onto the topside of a metal bar that was running along the low ceiling of the garage. Now he was ready to go.

Back at the house Reid went upstairs and grabbed a Kevlar vest and holster from the back of his closet before heading back downstairs to the laundry room. He opened the door of the built-in ironing board cabinet and pressed hard against the right side of the back panel. It clicked opened to reveal an array of guns and other small weapons. This was only a sample of his personal collection that was hidden throughout the house, but it had everything he would need for now. He selected a knife and two guns with extra ammo before restoring the cabinet. He was just walking back out to the garage as Aaron's motorcycle turned into the driveway.

"You made good time," Reid said when Aaron pulled off his helmet.

"Told you it wouldn't be hard," Aaron said as Reid started putting on his vest. "Jesus, man, your wound is bleeding."

"What?" Reid turned around best he could and saw the red staining his t-shirt. "Dammit, I must have pulled the stitches." He went out to the garage to grab his first-aid kit.

"A doctor should be looking at that," said Aaron.

"No time. You're going to have to help me."

Aaron bandaged it while he told Reid what he had learned. "So the car is registered to a Peter Maren, a suspected courier of local crime boss Aleksandr Morozov. Like anything else connected to the man, it hasn't been confirmed. But here's the thing; Morozov is Casimir's cousin."

"Do you think Morozov's helping him?" Reid asked as he grabbed a clean shirt from the laundry room and started again to gear up.

"Would make sense. But I know what you're thinking, and no, we have nothing concrete on Morozov to bring him in."

"Doesn't mean we can't question him."

Aaron shook his head. "The man is virtually untouchable. I think we'd be showing our hand by approaching him."

Reid thought about it and knew Aaron was right. Especially since they weren't working in any official capacity at the moment.

"You have an address for this Maren guy?" He asked.

"Of course."

Reid grabbed a water, an energy bar, and the bottle of ibuprofen sitting next to the fridge. "Let's head out then."

"How you wanna play this?" Aaron asked as

they sat in Reid's Cayenne. They parked on the street around the corner from Peter's apartment building in the Capitol Hill area of Seattle.

"I think I'll go in myself," said Reid. "If he tries to run, you can cut him off." He put in an earpiece and called Aaron's cell. "Keep the line open.

Aaron nodded and both men exited the vehicle. Reid made his way to the front while Aaron walked around the back, presumably keeping an eye out for other exits.

At the building entrance, Reid found a secured entry so he hung back a short distance until someone made their way to the door from the inside. He walked up and pretended to dig for a key. The couple leaving actually smiled at him as they held it open.

"Thanks," Reid said, returning the smile.

He took the elevator to the third floor and as he made his way down the hall, he noticed peep holes on the doors and knew that Peter wasn't going to be opening the door for Reid. He slowed down to listen for movement inside as he walked by and heard someone, hopefully Peter, on the other side of the door.

"Wells," he said quietly into the earpiece, "I'm pulling the fire alarm to draw him out. Let me know when help arrives."

"Copy that."

Reid continued to the end of the hallway and pulled on the lever, careful not to leave any fingerprints.

Most people were either not home or not taking the alarm seriously, because few tenants were exiting into the hallway, but Maren finally poked his head out to check the threat. Reid was ready, shoving him back inside and quickly aiming his gun to Maren's head as he kicked the door closed behind them.

Maren's mouth fell open. "You—you! I left you at the airport!"

"I'm glad you think so. Now, against the wall with your hands up." Maren did as he was told. "I'm going to ask you some questions, and if you want to make it out of this with all your body parts attached, then I suggest you answer them."

"You wouldn't shoot me here," said Maren. "Someone might hear you."

"First of all, I don't need a gun to dismember you. And second, in case you didn't notice, most of your neighbors are currently exiting the building. We have a few minutes until the fire department arrives. But I suggest you hurry, because when they do, you will no longer be of use to me. Now where is the girl?"

"What girl?"

Reid pressed the barrel harder against the back of Maren's head and cocked it.

"Oh, you mean that girl," he said. "I don't know where she is. They put her on a boat, but I don't know where they are going, I swear."

"What boat?" Reid asked, "Where would it

dock? You have to give me more, Maren."

"It's the boss's boat, the *Clara.*"

"And where does it usually dock?"

"I'm not sure."

Reid whacked the butt of his gun against the side of Maren's kneecap.

"Ow! I told you the truth. I don't know!"

"Then what do you know about it?"

"It's not in the lake. It's in the sound. Elliot Bay, I think."

Reid rolled his eyes. "Would it be the Elliot Bay Marina by any chance?"

Maren's eyes squinted shut, anticipating another blow. "I think so, I swear I don't know."

"Where's your phone?" Reid asked and Maren pointed to small table nearby. Reid pocketed it and then shot Maren in the knee. He'd live, but it would keep him busy long enough for Reid to get Jillian back. There was a fire escape out Maren's bedroom window. Reid's feet hit the ground right as engines were pulling up. He crossed the street and took the long way back to his car where Aaron was waiting.

"So now we just need to find this boat, the *Clara*?" he asked.

"We find the boat," said Reid. "We find Jillian."

The boat had left the dock over an hour ago and Jillian was seated on the couch, unsure what to do with herself. Now that they were out in the middle of the Puget Sound, she presumed Casimir wasn't worried about her escaping and seemed at ease as he conducted business in another language on his cell phone.

But that all changed with the arrival of a steward.

"Sir," he said holding out a phone, "Morozov is on the line for you."

"*Shcho*," Jillian heard Casimir answer.

He continued talking in the foreign tongue and Jillian tuned it out, but when he hung up, she couldn't help noticing that he looked pleased.

Without a word, Casimir grabbed Jillian by the arm and marched her across the room and down a flight of stairs, calling someone who followed them. Casimir opened a door and threw her in so hard that she fell onto the floor.

"*Steshyty za neyu!*" he ordered as he slammed the door shut and locked it.

Jillian stood up and pressed an ear to the door. Someone (she guessed Casimir) walked away while the other person remained on the other side of the door. She turned to survey the room, not much bigger than a broom closet. A small boring bed was in one corner and an even smaller bathroom in another.

It was hard to know exactly what was going on, but seeing as how Casimir suddenly felt the need to place her under lock and key, Jillian wondered if Reid was behind it. Was he keeping good on his promise to rescue her? Would he succeed?

[95]

Reid pushed a small Zodiac into the water from a boat ramp on the west side of San Juan Island and fired up the outboard motor. Using the GPS on his phone, he steered the boat in the direction where the *Clara* was sitting, just nosing the Washington-Canada border.

When Reid could plainly make out the boat's lights bobbing along the horizon, he cut the motor and took up the oars in an effort to draw as little attention as possible to himself. It was still a good twenty minutes of hard rowing before Reid reached the side of the *Clara*. He made for the darkest part of the boat and got as close to the railing as possible. Reid contemplated his next move. He was going to have to jump to grab the railing, and he was only going to have one chance at it, or he was in the water. One deep breath, and then Reid vaulted as high as he could. Both hands made contact with the metal bar, but one slipped just as he was tightening his grip. Now he hung off the yacht by a single arm that was already exhausted from the rowing. Another deep breath and Reid swung the free arm around, this time keeping hold. But he still needed to pull himself up over the railing. He was just about to do it when he heard footsteps coming in his direction. His only hope now was that they didn't see his fingers wrapped around the lowest railing. But then someone called out and the footsteps faded in the opposite direction. Reid summoned the last of his strength and climbed over the railing.

Now to figure where on the damn boat they were keeping Jillian. His best guess was that she was somewhere below. Quickly and quietly he made his way to the nearest door and found stairs leading to a lower deck with a narrow hall. Reid couldn't see what was at the other end of the hall, so he pulled out a small telescopic mirror and could see doors lining the hall, one of which was manned by someone with a gun. If they were guarding that room, that must be where Jillian was.

Reid screwed the silencer onto his pistol, wishing there was some other way. It was one thing shooting at someone firing you, but he had always hated this part of the job.

Jillian was inspecting the bathroom for anything that might help her out of this room when she heard a thump outside the door. She stepped out and could see the handle jiggling. She yanked the only lamp from the wall and positioned herself behind the door with it raised over her head. This might be her only chance—to do what she wasn't entirely sure, but she couldn't sit around waiting any longer.

There was a click and the handle was definitely turning now. Jillian sucked in a breath, preparing for whoever was coming through that door.

"Reid?" she said, certain her mind was playing tricks on her.

His familiar face beamed at her and Jillian's

hopes soared. He'd done it. He'd actually rescued her.

"How are you here?" she asked, lowering the lamp. "How is this possible? How do you *know* these people?" So many questions were going through her head; she didn't know where to start.

But Reid ignored her and wrapped his arms around her. "Thank God you're okay. Did they hurt you?" He pushed her out to arm's length, and Jillian saw his eyes settle on the cut lip. He frowned, but didn't comment on it.

"We have to get off this ship before anyone finds us," he said, pulling a gun from a holster, and for the first time she noticed the one already in his hand. "You know how to fire this, right?" he asked.

"Yes, but—"

"Good," he said, cutting her off. "I'm going to need you to stay close to me and shoot at anyone who isn't me." He peeked his head out the door and looked both ways. "With a little luck, we won't see anyone else."

Jillian looked at the floor by Reid's feet and saw the same man Casimir had posted guard at her door, now in a heap with a line of blood coming from the small hole in his forehead. His vacant eyes stared up at her. She shuddered.

"But how—" she started to ask, turning away from the gruesome sight.

"I promise I will answer all your questions later, but first we need to go now!" He pulled her out of the room with him and she tried to keep up as they headed down the hall, Reid's gun poised for a possible attack. Jillian looked down at the weapon in her hand and wondered if she would be able to use it. After all those hours in the gun range with her father, she never imagined she'd actually have to shoot a live target.

Movement caught her eye and she looked down the hall behind them just in time to see someone coming around the corner.

Shoot at anyone who isn't me.

"Reid!" she screamed, firing off a shot. Jillian missed by a mile, but it was enough to send him ducking for cover.

Reid spun her around, putting her in the lead, and pushed her forward as he fired back at whoever was still around that corner. Their attacker was sending bullets their way, but since he was too chicken to actually stick his head out, they weren't in any real danger. Yet.

"Everyone's going to know we're here now," said Reid. "Take the stairs, get out on the deck, and jump. I'll be right behind you."

"Jump in the water? That's your plan?"

"Just go!" he yelled without looking at her. Casimir's man had realized he needed a new tactic and stepped out into the hall. Jillian ran the last few feet up the steps, leaving Reid to provide cover. She bolted up the stairs and slammed right into a hard chest. She was immediately shoved against the wall. She could feel a hand trying to wrestle away the gun that was now lodged between their two bodies. Her other arm was being pinned by a death grip against her hip. Jillian held as tight to the gun as she could, but knew she didn't stand a chance against this much muscle. In one last-ditch effort she squeezed her fingers even tighter and jumped when the gun went off.

CHAPTER EIGHT

Reid raced up the stairs just in time to see Jillian struggling with another assailant and a split second later heard a gun go off. Both Jillian and her attacker froze, and Reid thought the worst.

"Oh, God, oh, God, please, no!"

But then the man slumped to the ground, almost taking Jillian with him. She managed to stay upright, looking like a deer caught in the headlights.

"I killed him," she whispered, looking at Reid. "I didn't mean to. I just—"

"It's okay," said Reid, grabbing her. "We have to go." He didn't have time to talk her down from this. There would be time enough for that if they could manage to get off this boat alive.

He poked his head out the door and could hear commotion all around, but it didn't sound close. Everyone was still trying to figure out what was going on, and this was their one small window to get off before anyone saw them.

Reid motioned Jillian to follow him out to the railing.

"So what do we do once we're in the water?" she whispered as they climbed over it.

"Stay close to the hull and wait for my direction. Ready?"

She nodded and they both jumped in.

Reid's head bobbed back to the surface to see Jillian already swimming towards the hull as instructed and he quickly joined her.

"Now what?" she asked, shivering.

He knew they couldn't spend too much time in the cold boundary waters.

"We find my raft," he said, pulling the phone from his vest pocket. Housed in a waterproof case, it told him that his raft carrying a tracking beacon had drifted thirty feet behind the boat. Further than he had hoped, but doable if they started moving now. "Swim this way, as quietly as you can," he told her.

Their hands had barely left the side of the yacht when he heard the motors kick on.

"Hurry," he said as a spotlight started searching the water. Reid could tell Jillian was fighting as hard as she could to stay with him, but she didn't have the same layers he did and the fear of hypothermia crept into his mind.

"We're almost there," he said, putting an arm around her waist, helping her to go faster. Her body relaxed and she stopped swimming, choosing to let him drag her.

"Jillian, honey, you've got to keep swimming. You need to keep your blood pumping."

She gave no sign that she had heard other than her legs kicking harder.

Panic was just starting to sweep through him when he slammed into the side of the black rubber craft. Reid tried lifting her into it first, but she didn't have the strength to get in and he couldn't get enough leverage to push her. Reluctantly he climbed in first and from there was able to pull her out of the water. Jillian collapsed on the bottom of the boat.

Reid pulled an emergency blanket out of a kit in the raft and looked towards the yacht, now moving in the opposite direction, still searching the waters with the bright light. He wrapped the blanket around Jillian who was conscious, but not saying anything. Her weak, ragged breathing was the only sign that she was still alive. The blanket would prevent her from losing any more body heat, but he knew she needed a heat source ASAP. He started the engine and steered the raft towards shore, making sure to keep plenty of distance from the boat.

When he was sure they had enough ground, or water in this case, between them, Reid called Aaron.

"She's safe," he said as soon as Aaron answered. "Leak the intel and assemble a team.

"Got it," Aaron said and hung up.

Now that Jillian was out of harm's way, Reid

felt comfortable alerting the authorities of Casimir's whereabouts without risking her becoming collateral damage.

"Talk to me, Jillian," he said.

"About what?" she asked through chattering teeth.

"Anything. I just need you to stay awake."

"I'm too cold to fall asleep right now," she said.

"That's a good sign. We'll get you warmed up as soon as we get to shore."

"Why aren't you balled up down here, feeling like an icicle?"

"I have a wetsuit jacket on," he said. "Trust me, I'm still feeling the chill, but I haven't lost as much body heat as you."

"Can I ask questions now?"

"Yes," he said.

"How do you know that man? Casimir."

Reid was trying to think how best to answer that when she asked another question.

"You don't work in bank security, do you?"

"No, I don't."

"Is your name even Reid Jackson?" she asked.

Reid could hear the distrust in her voice.

"Yes, Jillian, my name really is Reid," he said. "Hold on, we're coming to shore."

Jillian felt the thud before she had a chance to lift her head. Reid was out of the boat in an instant, pulling it onto dry land. She started to push up to see where they were, but then he was scooping her out of the boat, still wrapped in the aluminum blanket. Instead of taking in her surroundings, Jillian buried her head into his neck. It felt only slightly warmer than her own chilled flesh. In less than a minute Reid was laying her in the back seat of the SUV before opening the driver's door and starting the vehicle. She could hear air blasting and prayed that it warmed up quickly; even her bones ached from the cold.

"We have to get you out of these wet clothes," he said, climbing into the back seat with her. Jillian let Reid help her sit up and start removing her sopping wet clothes. She heard the sloshing noise as he tossed them into the back of the vehicle. When she was down to her bra and underwear, Reid pulled off some of his own layers, and she could feel his warm chest pressed against hers as he pulled the blanket over both of them.

"You never answered my first question," she said. "How do you know Casimir? Why did he kidnap me?"

"Anton Casimir is an international criminal. Last week when I said I was in New York, I was actually in Mexico City saving another man and keeping sensitive information out of Casimir's hands. He took you hoping that he could force me to get that information back in exchange for you."

"But why me?" she asked. "Why did he think he could use me?"

"Somehow he knew," Jillian felt Reid swallow hard before continuing, "he knew I cared enough about you that I wasn't going to just walk away."

"But *how*?"

Reid shook his head. "I haven't figured it out yet. But it turns out you were right that night you felt like somebody was watching you."

"That doesn't make any sense," Jillian said, sitting up straight, and Reid immediately pulled her back into him. "We had barely met, you didn't even ask me out until later that night. Why would he single me out from all the other neighbors?"

"I don't know. *I* hadn't even heard of Casimir at that point. Which means there has to be an inside man."

"But why me?" Jillian muttered. She just couldn't wrap her head around it.

"I'll figure it out eventually, but first we need to get you somewhere safe. Are you feeling warmer yet?"

Jillian still felt a chill, but it didn't hurt anymore.

"A little," she said.

"Good. You stay here in the warm car while I deflate the raft and load it."

He pulled away from her, and Jillian wished she had lied about being warmer. "All right."

Sitting alone in the back seat under the blanket, Jillian replayed everything Reid had just told her. First off, he wasn't who he said he was. Second, because he had shown interest in her—what was it he said—cared about her, a dangerous man had decided to abduct her and hold her ransom for something apparently only Reid could get. She thought of their dinner in Seattle and remembered how reluctant he had been to talk about himself. Was it because of his double life? And then she remembered their conversation at the Falls. Had any of that been real? Had he made up the story about his parents just to have something to talk about? She was confused. But then she remembered that Reid had just risked his life to save her, had killed at least one man to get her off that boat. She thought at least some of that had have been sincere. And then Jillian thought of the man *she* had killed and wondered how long that would haunt her.

Reid opened the valve on the Zodiac to let it deflate while he carried his gear bag and the small outboard motor to his SUV.

"How you doing, Jillian?" he asked with the tailgate open.

"Fine," she said, without looking back at him.

Knowing she was far from fine, Reid grabbed the carry bag for the boat and walked back over to roll the last of the air out and pack it up as quickly as possible. He could see a light off in the distance headed in their direction and guessed it to be the *Clara.* It was going to take a couple hours before Aaron could convince their superiors that Casimir was in the area without giving away how he and Reid knew. They just needed to buy some time.

Reid slammed the tailgate and slid into the driver's seat.

"We need to find somewhere to rest a couple hours until the first ferry out," he said twisting back to look at her. "It's warmer up here, but if you want to lay down back there, that's fine too."

Without answering she proceeded to climb over the console into the seat next to him, bringing the blanket with her.

"We'll figure out how to get you some dry clothes," he said.

She nodded, still not speaking.

A glance in the rear view mirror showed a yacht coming closer. Not that it could get to the shallow shore here, but Reid drove off as quickly as possible anyway.

Reid kept glancing at Jillian, who stared straight ahead, barely making any movements. The silence was killing him.

"It's going to be okay," he said, reaching for a hand that was poking from beneath the blanket. "You're safe now."

She finally looked at him, giving his hand a small squeeze.

"Thank you," she said.

"For what?"

"For coming to get me."

"Of course," he said.

They rode another mile through the dark in silence, her hand still in his, but Reid could almost hear the wheels turning in her head.

"Who *do* you work for?" she asked.

"I work for the government," he said. "That's all I can really tell you right now."

"So you're like a spy?"

"Sort of," he said with a smile. "A true spy as you are imagining is someone who goes in and gathers information. I'm more the agent that goes into action based on that information."

"You mean a clandestine agent?" she asked. "Like in the movies?"

"Exactly."

"How did you end up living in the suburbs?"

"It was quiet. Living in a proper house made me feel a little more normal when I wasn't out in the field."

"I see," she said.

"Do you?" he asked.

"Honestly, no. I feel like this is all just a bad dream. And any minute now I'm going to wake up and—and I don't know."

"It's a lot to take in. And it will be easier once you get some rest."

He pulled into the parking lot of a small motel.

"I'll see if they have a room for us. Be right back."

After waking a very irritated manager, Reid

walked back with a room key and moved the vehicle closer to their room so Jillian wouldn't have as far to walk with nothing but the blanket covering her. Fortunately not many people were about this time of night.

CHAPTER NINE

Reid opened the door to the room and let Jillian enter first. The decor was depressing with its wood paneled walls, but it was clean and had a bed, which was all she needed right now. She walked to the middle of it and pulled the blanket tighter around, trying to decide what to do with herself.

"I think I need a shower," she said.

Reid nodded. "I saw a vending machine by the office. I'm going to grab some snacks. I have the key so don't open the door if anybody knocks."

Are we still not safe? Jillian shuddered.

"Okay," she said.

He stepped out and she went into the bathroom. The room felt sterile with the white fixtures and walls; even the towels and tiny bars of soap were lacking any color.

She let the blanket fall to the floor, avoiding

the mirror for fear of what she might see, and turned on the water. Her hand went to the split lip and she wondered if it looked as ugly as it felt.

The hot water was still pouring down her body when she heard the door open. She couldn't help but hold her breath until Reid called out. Just knowing he was in the room made her feel safer.

Jillian finished rinsing off, wrapped a towel around, and braced herself to stand in front of the mirror.

The lip wasn't as bad as she had expected. It was swollen, but only slightly, and the cut looked a lot smaller than it felt beneath her touch. Her gaze moved on to the fingertip-shaped bruises on her arm. She was looking at the larger one on her back when Reid came in to check on her.

She stared at his reflection in the mirror and could see the anger and guilt swirling in his eyes. He set a red pouch on the back of the toilet before standing directly behind her, and gently touched the bruise.

"I'm so sorry," he whispered and leaned forward to kiss it. Jillian closed her eyes as the warmth of his lips spread through her body like some magic tonic that could make all the aches and fear go away.

He lifted his lips and Jillian opened her eyes to see Reid's own scrapes and bruises for the first time. She soaked a washcloth with warm water and turned to face him. Red was staining the sleeve of his shirt, and she carefully lifted the material to wipe away the dried blood, revealing what she imagined to be the graze from a bullet. She pushed his shirt up and he took over, pulling it off over his head. As he tossed it onto the floor, she saw more blood on the shirt.

A quick look revealed no other wounds on his torso, so she craned her neck until she saw the soaked bandage peeling back, exposing stitches on his lower back, some of which had started to give.

"What happened?" she asked, facing him again.

"I was shot in Mexico," he said. "By Casimir's men."

"Is this normal for you? To be shot at?"

He nodded, taking the washcloth from her hand and tossing it into the sink before kissing her hard.

Jillian wrapped her arms around his neck and felt his embrace tighten.

The towel around her loosened when she lifted her arms and a gentle tug from Reid brought it down completely.

Thoughts of the last twenty-four hours disappeared as Jillian became aware of Reid's flesh upon her own. But it wasn't enough. She wanted to be lost in him completely.

"Please," she breathed, pulling away from him.

At first Reid thought she was asking him to

stop, but then realized her hands were at the waistband of his still damp pants, working at the zipper. Ignoring the erection that was building behind it, he grabbed her wrists, stopping her.

"You're exhausted and confused right now," he said, trying to even out his breathing. "I don't think this is what you really want."

Jillian looked him square in the eye. "Don't tell me what I want."

Reid's gaze moved down to her parted lips. He watched the muscles in her neck flex as she swallowed. Before he could make up his mind though, she wrested her hands from his grip and pulled his mouth to hers. Reid didn't bother arguing, because the truth was he wanted this just as bad, maybe more so.

Cupping her ass, he lifted Jillian up onto the small counter space between sink and wall. With lips still locked, Reid took hold of a bare breast, rubbing his left thumb over the hard peak, and he felt her nails gently score his chest.

He pulled her into him with his free hand while moving his mouth down her neck and torso to the teased nipple, flicking his tongue across it. A moan escaped her lips as she raked her fingers though his hair and the bulge in his pants tightened that much more. He slid the hand on her back down her right thigh and back up between her legs while his mouth traced a path back to her lips. His hand reached the soft nest of curls and stroked her softly with his thumb. Her body shuddered in response and she wrapped her legs around him, trying to pull his body closer to hers.

Not that it was going to do her much good with these pants still on. Reid untangled himself from her to remove them and as he stood naked in front of Jillian, equally unclothed, he caressed her cheek. She reached up to touch his hand and he saw the bruise on her arm. Again he looked at the bruise on her back, reflected by the mirror behind her.

"I'm sorry," he told her one more time.

"I don't blame you for what's happened," she said with a frown, but it quickly disappeared. "Now shut up and finish what you've started."

Reid jerked involuntarily as she enveloped his dick in her hand. He was sure she could feel it throbbing against her hot grip. Kissing her, he took both her hands and placed them around his neck before lifting her off the counter and she locked her legs around him.

He carried her to other room and dropped her onto the bed, causing her to giggle. Lifting her left leg, he kneeled on the foot of the bed and pressed his lips to the top of her knee, and Jillian's fingers dug into the comforter. Ever so slowly he skimmed the warm, silky flesh until his mouth reached where his thumb had been only moments before, and she moaned as he began to lick at her. He felt the heel of her raised leg dig into his back, urging him on. He sucked harder and she gave a tiny little scream.

Reid stopped and pulled back. He wanted to be

inside her the first time she came for him.

There was a whimper of disappointment, but she combed her fingers through his hair as he slowly, gently kissed a path up her abdomen. He stopped at one mound of flesh to flick his tongue across one nipple, then suck on the other. She was writhing impatiently beneath him, her hands desperately tugging at him, trying to bring his face closer. He pushed up and stared into her beautiful brown eyes, searching again for permission. As much as he wanted to keep going and pretend that tomorrow would never come, he needed to be sure that this was what she really wanted. In answer she lifted her head to nip at his lower lip, giving a devilish grin as she fell back down. He leaned in close to tug at her earlobe with his teeth as he started to slide into her. She bucked her hips, plunging him even deeper, and Reid's breath caught in his throat.

She moaned and he could feel the vibrations of it against his jaw.

As he moved in and out of her, slowly at first, then with more urgency, he could feel her breath quickening, becoming even more ragged, and knew she was close.

Suddenly Jillian's hand flew to her mouth just as she was tightening around him and Reid took hold of the hand, pinning it over her head so that she had no choice but to completely let go. Her chest lifted off the bed and she threw her head back as the most erotic scream ruptured from her throat.

He continued to pound into her, could still feel her body convulsing, until the orgasm finally subsided. Reid slowed the pace, but it wasn't long until she was urging him on again by flexing her palms against his ass and he obliged with enthusiasm. After yet another wave wracked through her body, Reid was unable to hold back his own climax any longer. As she wrapped her legs around even tighter than he thought possible, he felt every ounce of strength he had pouring into her.

When his senses finally returned, Reid looked down at Jillian. Her damp hair was matted to her sweaty face and she was looking at him with complete and utter satisfaction.

He started to roll on to the bed next to her when a pain in his back reminded him of the failing stitches.

"Be right back," he said, kissing Jillian's forehead.

He climbed out of bed and went into the bathroom where he grabbed the first-aid kit from the back of the toilet. It had been his reason for coming in here earlier, before getting distracted.

There wasn't much he could do for the wound at the moment, but he slapped a new bandage on it, if only to keep it as clean as possible until a doctor could get to it.

Reid walked back out to find Jillian asleep under the covers. He set the alarm on his phone and crawled in next to her, wishing that they were in his bed, and that she had never heard of Anton Casimir.

"Jillian. Time to wake up."

She opened her eyes to find Reid sitting in the room's solitary chair next to the bed.

"Good morning," she smiled. When he didn't return it, she frowned and asked, "How long have you been up?"

"A while." He stood and held out a bag. "There was a twenty-four hour Laundromat nearby and I was able to dry your clothes. They're in the bathroom."

She accepted it, feeling a little put off by his cold demeanor. Did she dream last night? In the bag she found a comb, travel toothbrush and toothpaste.

"We need to get to the ferry," he said.

She started to get out of bed, but found herself embarrassed of her nudity in light of his new attitude. She grabbed the coverlet and wrapped it around her body to walk to the bathroom where she freshened up as best she could.

"Ready to go?" Reid asked when she came out.

"I guess."

The sky was still black as they walked out to the car and Reid placed his hand on the small of her back to help her in.

He was just about to close the door when Jillian asked him if everything was alright.

"Yes. Why?"

She searched his face looking for some clue as to why he was so distant now, but it gave nothing away.

"Never mind," she said, shaking her head.

"We just need to get moving," he said and closed the door.

The drive to the ferry terminal was silent and it only deepened Jillian's unease.

"Did you sleep last night?" she asked when they joined the other cars waiting for the first sailing of the day.

"A little bit."

"Where did you sleep?"

In the reflection of the dash lights, she could see his face soften, though he continued to stare ahead.

"In the bed. Next to you." But then he frowned and finally looked at her. "Where did you think I slept?"

"I wasn't sure. It just—it just feels like you're avoiding me now."

Reid faced forward again and heaved a sigh. "Oh, Jillian. You have no idea."

That was an understatement.

"I almost forgot," Reid said as reached around to the back seat, grabbing the snacks he had bought from the vending machine while Jillian was showering. "You fell asleep so quickly after…last night that you didn't get a chance to eat. You should probably eat something soon."

"Thanks," Jillian muttered as she opened a granola bar and bit off a chunk while she thought about *last night*. Was it just a moment of weakness for Reid? Did he regret it already? As she chewed on the bar that tasted more like cardboard at the moment, she started to wonder how *she* felt about last night. Maybe it had been a moment of weakness for Jillian as well, but she was sure she didn't regret it.

They sat in silence until the lights of the ferry bobbed across the water as it made its approach to the terminal.

As though reading her thoughts, Reid looked at her and said, "I'm glad last night happened, Jillian."

She stared back at him.

"Just in case you were wondering," he explained. "Last night was amazing, and right now all I want to do is take you home and do it all over again. But I need to focus on keeping you safe until Casimir is dealt with."

"What do you mean?" she asked.

"Before I came for you, I sent your father to a cabin I own outside of Lake Stevens. You're going to drop me off in Everett where I can take the train back to Seattle and then I want you to meet him at the cabin and wait until it's safe.

"You're not coming with me?"

"I can't," Reid said, shaking his head. "It might look suspicious if I don't show up today."

"Why would it look suspicious? Were you not supposed to help me?"

Reid shook his head.

"I wasn't important enough for them to go after the bastard," she said somberly.

"We're going after him, but I couldn't risk you getting hurt in the crossfire."

Jillian watched the cars in front of them start to move forward and then they too were preparing to board the ferry. She may not have been important enough for whoever Reid worked for, but she was to him.

"It's a couple hours until we're in Everett," he told her as they drove onto the ship and a ferry worker directed them to a lane. "With a little luck, they'll have him by the time I get in."

"And what if they don't?"

Reid killed the engine and took her hand. "Then at least I know you're somewhere safe, somewhere he would never think to look for you." He kissed the hand he was holding. "Now do you want to go upstairs and see if they are serving food yet, or should we stay here and you can take a nap?"

Jillian looked at the half-eaten bar sitting in her lap. Maybe there was something more appetizing upstairs.

"Let's go," she said.

Reid pulled up to the train station and left the engine running.

"How long until we can go home?" Jillian asked.

[121]

"If everything goes well, you'll be sleeping in your own bed by tomorrow. Worst case, a couple of days. I just need to know that you're safe until we have him in custody."

She nodded.

"And then what happens?" she asked.

He leaned across the seat and cupped her face. "Then I think I take you on a date that finally ends the way we want."

"I'd like that a lot," she said with a smile.

They both climbed out and Reid kissed her before letting her slip behind the wheel.

"I'll call you as soon as I have word," he said, handing her his cell phone.

"Be safe," she said.

"I will." He gave her one last kiss before closing the car door and watched her drive off.

Reid walked into the agency and found Aaron standing at his desk talking to fellow agent Gavin Maxwell, both looking defeated.

"What's going on?" asked Reid.

"We received intel that Casimir was on a boat off Friday Harbor," said Aaron, not quite meeting Reid's eye.

"Really? That's great," said Reid, pretending he didn't already know this.

"Unfortunately," said Gavin, "by the time we raided it, he was gone."

Reid's blood ran cold. "What do you mean?

Are you telling me he wasn't on it?"

Gavin shook his head. "He could still be in the state, or he may have crossed the border into Canada. Relax, Jackson," he said, putting a hand on Reid's shoulder, "Casimir was stupid enough to show up in our own backyard. He'll mess up again, and this time we'll be ready."

Gavin removed his hand and sauntered off, having no idea what it meant that Casimir was still out there.

"How can you have no idea where he is?" Reid growled. "He was practically gift wrapped!"

"He was off the damn boat by the time you got to it, Jackson. This isn't our fault!"

Reid dropped down into Aaron's chair. Why would Casimir leave and not take Jillian with him?

"One of the crew members told us that after Casimir got a call from Morozov," Aaron explained, "he took the girl downstairs and arranged for transportation off the boat.

"Did he say where Casimir went?" asked Reid

"He didn't know," Aaron said, shaking his head. "Apparently a tender came and got him and that's the last they saw of him."

Reid put his head in his hands trying to think.

"I'm sorry, man," said Aaron, "I don't know what to tell you. Casimir is obviously smarter than we give him credit for."

Reid raised his head. "There has to be a mole."

"No way," said Aaron. "Our team is solid."

"But Casimir knows too much. He has to have an inside man somewhere. He was watching Jillian almost from the moment I met her."

"Who here knows about Jillian other than me? This doesn't sound like anything from our end."

Reid looked up at Aaron. He was right, no one but Aaron knew about Jillian. It wasn't possible. This was the man who had saved Reid's skin countless times. But what if?

"Are you sure she's safe at your cabin?" Aaron asked.

And Aaron was the only person who knew he had sent Jillian and her father to the cabin.

"I don't know," Reid said, frowning at Aaron. "Maybe I should move them."

Aaron gave Reid a strange look, but before he could say anything, Director Rollins walked by.

"There you are, Agent Jackson. I see Riker left a stack of paperwork for you," she said, looking at Reid's nearby desk.

"I was just about to get started on it," said Reid. "But first I need to run down and have medical look at my stitches. Think I might have pulled them."

"Why doesn't that surprise me?" she asked, shaking her head as she continued on her way.

He mustered a smile at Aaron before striding off. But he didn't go to medical. Two floors down, Reid requested the use of a cell phone and one of the company sedans. He needed to get to Jillian before anyone else did.

The sun was at its highest point when Jillian pulled up to the cabin. It was small and old, but appeared to be well maintained. Her father came rushing out to her before she even had a chance to kill the engine and Jillian couldn't remember the last time she had been so happy to see him.

"Oh, Papa," she said as he embraced her.

"Jillian, I'm so sorry."

"It's okay Papa, I'm here."

"My *Tesoro*, please forgive me," he said and Jillian realized he was crying.

"What's going on?" she asked, pulling away. "Forgive you for what?"

"I hoped you would never be involved," Jacob said with tears streaming down his face.

The screen door slammed and Jillian looked up to see Casimir step out onto the covered porch.

CHAPTER TEN

"Papa," Jillian said, looking from Casimir to her father's guilty expression, "what have you done?"

He shook his head without answering and two armed men stepped out of the cottage and escorted Jillian and her father into the cabin's cozy living room, instructing them to sit on the tartan couch. Another man with similar features of Casimir, though much younger, walked into the room.

"Isn't this a nice family reunion," he said. Jillian was surprised when he didn't speak with the same thick accent as Casimir. In fact, if she hadn't been expecting it, searching for it, she was sure that she wouldn't have heard one at all.

"Who are you?" she asked.

"Normally I might be insulted," the man said as he settled into a nearby chair, "but I imagine your father has wanted to keep our longtime association a secret from you."

At his words, Jacob gave a sob and wiped his cheek with the back of his hand.

"Is this true?" she asked, looking at him, but he avoided her glare.

"When we lost your mother, I was a mess," he said. "I was about to lose everything, including you." He reached for her hand without looking up, but she pulled it away.

Jillian looked up to Casimir, leaning against the mantle, distractedly cleaning out the dirt from a fingernail, then to the other man, who was clearly amused by all this.

"My father helped your father," he pointed to Jacob, "get back on his feet. Helped him to bring his precious daughter home."

"In exchange for what?" Jillian asked. "What did you agree to, Papa?"

"It was my position with Boeing," Jacob said, his head hung in shame. "Specifically, the military defense sector."

"You didn't?" she gasped. "Tell me you didn't sell military secrets to these people." But he didn't need to answer. "Who are you?" she said to her father, who covered his face in his hands.

Casimir, finally showing interest, gave a chuckle.

"But how does Reid play into this?"

"That, my dear," said Casimir's associate, opening his palms to the heavens, "was just fate bestowing her good fortune upon us. Thanks to an associate of mine, the name of an agent, Reid Jackson, happened to come into my possession. So I bought your father a nice house right across the street. To keep an eye on him, see if anything useful might turn up."

"That's why you moved," she said. Jillian had always assumed it was too many painful memories at the old house.

"But when you, Jacob's own daughter, caught the eye of Agent Jackson, well, it was like winning the lottery."

"And that's how you knew to put surveillance in my house," she said.

The man nodded. "I always knew the day would come when you discovered your father's true nature," he said. "I wanted to be here first hand to see the look on your face."

There was a perverse pleasure in his smile, and for the first time, Jillian noticed he was wearing a wedding ring. She wondered what woman had married this man.

"But if you don't mind," he said, getting up from the chair, "I think I'll leave before things get too messy."

"And now what?" Jillian asked Casimir as the man walked out.

"Now we wait for Jackson to call," said Casimir.

As Reid drove north, he called his own cell phone, hoping Jillian would answer the blocked call showing on her end. The call was answered, but it wasn't Jillian.

"Agent Jackson, I assume," said Casimir and Reid felt his blood begin to boil.

"Where's Jillian?" he asked.

"Do not worry. She is fine," said Casimir. "For now."

"What do you want? Is this really about those codes?"

"Come and join us. Then we will discuss that I want. But come alone. And I suggest you hurry, I am beginning to grow bored of this game."

The line went dead and Reid slammed the phone against the dash repeatedly until it finally broke. He'd have to pay the agency back for it, but he didn't really give a fuck about it right now.

Tossing the smashed pieces on the seat next to him, Reid pressed harder on the accelerator. He knew he was walking into a no-win situation, but he also knew he couldn't leave Jillian to whatever Casimir had in store for her.

Reid was on his way, but Jillian wasn't entirely sure how that was going to help them. He had lost the element of surprise, and she was pretty sure Casimir and his men weren't going to let him walk in here armed. It was up to her to find something, anything that might help increase their odds of walking away from this alive.

"I have to go to the bathroom," she said.

Casimir looked up from his phone with a raised eyebrow.

"*Viz'-mit yi-yi*," he said to the bald guard who had remained inside when the other two went outside to wait for Reid.

Baldie led her through the kitchen and into a small bathroom that had no window.

"Go fast," he said in stuttered English.

Jillian closed the door behind her and quietly turned the lock, if only for a false sense of security, and looked through the cabinet. Everything in it was what you'd expect to find in a bathroom, and even then there wasn't much. It didn't take long to realize nothing here would be useful. She stood up and considered what she knew about Reid. With an occupation like his, surely he was prepared for anything, had a weapon stashed everywhere.

A pounding at the door made her jump.

"Hurry," said Baldie from the other side of it.

Jillian sighed. So much for her bright idea. She flushed the toilet for good measure and walked over to the sink, turning on the faucet. Needing a minute to brace herself before facing Casimir and her father again, Jillian gripped the small counter and heaved a sigh. As she put all her weight against the vanity, what she thought was a false drawer front, previously immovable, now sprung open a crack. She pried it open further and found exactly what she was looking for: a small-caliber handgun. With trembling fingers, she removed it and slid it into the waistband of her jeans as Baldie pounded even harder on the door.

Jillian turned off the water and opened the door.

"What take so long?" Baldie asked.

"I'm sorry, I have to pee when I'm nervous," she said, and moved back into the living room to wait for Reid and the perfect opportunity.

Reid pulled into the driveway to see two AK-47s aimed at him.

"Put your hands up," a blonde-haired muscle shouted when Reid had stopped the car. Reid did as he asked. The door was opened for him to climb out while the other guy did a walk around the car, making sure that Reid had indeed come unaccompanied. When he was satisfied, he patted Reid down as predicted while the blonde kept the muzzle pointed at Reid's head.

"Come," the blonde ordered when they found nothing on him.

Jillian was feeling the loose spring in the couch when she heard gravel crunching in the driveway and her heart leapt. It had to be Reid.

The clock over the fireplace ticked away the seconds as Jillian waited for him to come through the front door, and when he did with hands up and two gunned men flanking him, she felt defeated. What chance did her one pistol have against these men's weapons? There was no way they were all walking out alive, if any of them.

"Sit," Casimir ordered from where he was still standing by the fireplace, cutting the end off of a cigar.

Reid moved to sit next to her, but one of the other men used the end of his gun to direct him to a chair across the room where the other man had sat not so long ago.

"All right," Reid said as he sat down, giving a Jillian a quick glance. "I'm here. But you're wasting your time because you'll never get those codes, even if I could get my hands on them."

"This was never about the codes," said Casimir and Jillian watched confusion come over Reid's face. "I knew that was a lost cause once Davies went into protection."

"Then why take Jillian? Why come after me? Are you looking for revenge?"

Casimir cocked an eyebrow. "You think I would waste my time on something as petty as revenge?" He sat down on the couch next to Jillian and lit his cigar. She tried to scoot away from him, but didn't have much room with her father taking up the other end of the small couch.

"You have something that may be just as valuable as a transponder and the codes to go with it." Casimir puffed on the cigar before continuing. Jillian felt his arm slide along the back of the couch behind her, making her recoil, and when he exhaled in her face she turned her nose away.

"Don't you—" Reid started, jumping out of his chair, but was interrupted by the butt of a gun to his abdomen. Jillian gasped and Casimir laughed.

"That is what I was hoping for," said Casimir, leaning forward to flick his cigar on the reclaimed wood coffee table. "You see, Agent Jackson. This whole exercise has been about finding out just how much Miss Sandro means to you. How far are you willing to go to keep her safe?"

Reid's face went white, but Jillian still wasn't following.

"You won't turn me," said Reid. "You have to know I would never work for you."

"Oh, nothing as complicated as that," said Casimir. "I do not have the patience to keep tabs on rats the way," he looked across Jillian to her father, "Mr. Sandro's benefactor does."

Baldie walked into the room and handed a hefty laptop to Casimir.

"It is simple," Casimir said, sliding the laptop across the coffee table towards Reid. "I want you to log into your mainframe and let me download as much data as you have access to."

And now Jillian understood. She was the bait. Casimir was asking Reid to trade her life for classified secrets. She looked at her father, who had already gone down this route, and then back to Reid, who appeared to be considering it.

"You can't, Reid."

Reid looked up from the computer to her and Casimir laughed.

"How sweet," he said. "She thinks it will be that easy, doesn't she?"

And now there was anguish in Reid's eyes. Why was he even considering it?

"I won't let you be a traitor like my father." But Reid was shaking his head as she spoke. "He'll just have to kill me now."

Jillian had forgotten about Casimir's arm behind her until it grabbed a fistful of hair. She screamed as he yanked her head back so fast she thought her neck would snap.

Reid tried to jump up again, only to be stopped with another blow, this time to his back. He fell forward onto the ground. Her cowardly father begged Casimir to let her go, but his words were barely audible.

"You see, Miss Sandro," Casimir growled into her ear, "death would be a treat compared to what I could do to you."

"I'll do it," Reid said, and Casimir released Jillian. She could see blood spotting his shirt where the stitches were as he climbed back up into the chair.

Jillian got up and walked around the table to him without anyone attempting to stop her.

"You can't," she said, crouching down beside him so as not to expose the gun on her back. "I'm not worth it. And who's to say he isn't going to kill us all anyway."

Reid stood, pulling her up with him, and brushed the hair from her face. She had never seen him look so sad.

"There are things worse than death," he said. "And he's not afraid to go there."

"It doesn't matter," she said. "Whether we live or die, we can't give this man what he wants."

"But he's right. I won't watch him torture you."

"Enough time for this touching scene," said Casimir. "Step out of the way, Miss Sandro."

"Then watch my back," she said, and had to refrain from smiling at the baffled look on his face. Jillian turned around and snatched the laptop, hugging it to her chest.

"Jillian," Reid sighed, clearly not happy with her action.

"You think that will stop me?" Casimir laughed, just as Jillian had hoped. He didn't see her as a threat by grabbing the computer, and she was able to get a couple steps distance between herself and everyone.

"Give me the laptop before I take it from you," he warned.

She reached behind for the gun and pointed it right at Casimir.

"Jesus Christ, Jillian!" Reid called out.

"You'll have to kill me to get it," she said. "And then you lose all leverage over Reid."

"A little girl like you isn't going to shoot me," said Casimir taking a stride towards her with his arms out.

"Like hell, I won't," she said and sent a bullet into the floor between his feet. Her aim was much better at this distance. It was enough to stop him in his tracks. It was also enough to point the other two big guns her direction, and she gave Reid a look that didn't take him long to read.

In one swift movement, he took control of the gun closest to him, sent an elbow to the face of the man it was attached to, and got a shot off hitting the second gunned man before aiming it at the third man, whose gun was aimed right back at him.

"And what the hell did that accomplish?" Casimir asked, fuming. "If you shoot me, your precious Reid will die."

"My man is prepared to die for his country," she said, "as am I. Are you?" But deep down Jillian knew he was right. They were still at the same standoff as before, just a few less players. Truth was she really didn't want to die today. And she didn't want to lose Reid either.

But then the glass from a window shattered and the last gunman dropped, causing Jillian to panic. Her confusion must have been enough for Casimir because he knocked her to the ground in an instant, trying to wrestle the gun from her. Jillian felt it slipping from her grasp just as Casimir cried out in pain. As he rolled off of her, clutching his side, she saw Reid standing over them taking another kick at Casimir. She slid away, still holding the gun, trying to avoid the mess when Aaron barged in through the front door and stopped Reid from taking any more blows at him.

As Aaron zip tied Casimir's wrist, Reid helped Jillian to her feet.

"Are you okay?" he asked, checking her face and body for any marks.

"I'm fine," she said. The scuffle hadn't been that bad.

"What the hell were you thinking? You could have gotten yourself killed!"

"He was going to kill us either way, wasn't he?"

He pulled her against his chest and Jillian wrapped her arms around his midsection. Was it really over? She looked at Casimir, still on the floor with his hands bound behind his back. Aaron was on the phone calling in to someone when movement in the far corner of the room caught her eye. Her father was huddled there, crying again.

"You!" she cried, pushing away from Reid. "This is your fault!"

She had marched half-way across the room when Reid's arms caught her by the waist, preventing her from getting any closer to him.

"You fucking coward!" she screamed, trying to push Reid's arms off of her, but now he was keeping her feet from even touching the ground.

"I'm sorry," he father sobbed as he pushed himself up to standing. "After your mother died ..."

"Don't you bring her into this! She would have been ashamed of you. How dare you!"

Reid carried her to the door as she still struggled against him.

"Restrain him as well," Reid said to Aaron as they walked out of the cabin where he finally set her down on the gravel.

"My own father," she said, turning around to face him. "How could he?"

Instead of answering, Reid again pulled her into him and this time she started crying into his chest. It was all too much. The abduction, the standoff, her father's betrayal.

"For the past ten years he's been lying to me," she muttered into Reid's shirt and he rubbed her back, still not speaking. And then she remembered that her father wasn't the only one who had been keeping secrets. She lifted her head and looked into the blue eyes that had always been so intimidating.

"Please don't look at me like that," said Reid.

"I guess I don't really know any of the people in my life, do I? Not Cameron, not my father. Not even you."

"It's not the same with me."

"Isn't it?" she asked. "Half of what you've told me has been a lie. Where you work, where you go when you're not here."

"But I've never lied about how I feel about

you. And I would never willingly put you in danger."

Jillian didn't doubt Reid's words, not after everything they had just gone through, but she was so confused right now.

"I love you," he whispered, as though sensing her thoughts.

The screen door creaked and they both looked up to see Aaron coming out.

"A team should be here in about thirty minutes," he said.

Jillian stepped back from Reid, and with Aaron witnessing, he let her go.

"Can I go home now?" she asked.

"Afraid not," Aaron told her. "They're going to want to talk to you."

She looked at Reid who nodded.

"I'm sorry," he said.

"I'll wait in the car," she said and trudged over to Reid's SUV.

As she crawled into the passenger seat, she thought of Reid's proclamation and felt bad for leaving him hanging. Deep down she knew she felt the same way, but wondered if it was enough.

Reid watched Jillian climb into the car. He knew she needed time. What she would decide to do after that, he didn't know.

"Apology accepted, by the way," said Aaron.

Reid looked at him. "For what?"

"For suspecting me."

Unable to look him in the eye, Reid looked down at the dirt.

"How did you know?" he asked.

"I saw the look on your face. And because I would've come to the same conclusion based on the evidence."

"I wanted to be wrong," Reid said, finally meeting Aaron's eye. "I'm glad I was wrong. What made you decide to come up here?"

"I figured it was where you were headed," said Aaron. "And if you were right about someone leaking information, there was a good chance you were going to need back-up. Just because you doubted me didn't mean I was going to leave you high and dry."

"I'm sorry, man. I don't know what to say."

"Like I said. Apology accepted. So what are we going to tell the Director when she gets here?" Aaron asked.

"The truth," Reid told him.

"You sure?"

Reid looked at Jillian sitting in his vehicle.

"Yes. No more lies."

For the next half-hour, Jillian watched Aaron and Reid from the car. Occasionally Aaron would step into the cabin and come right back out. She figured he was checking on Casimir and Jacob. From out here it was easy to forget that her father was inside, restrained and waiting for the authorities. She wondered what would happen to him, but wasn't ready to ask that question.

Reid kept looking back at her, frowning, and it made her heart ache. She was just about to open the door and go talk to him when a black SUV pulled up and several people jumped out. A dark sedan came in right behind it and someone opened the back door for a woman to climb out. She was dressed in a smart black pantsuit and expensive, but practical shoes.

"You've got some explaining to do, Agent Jackson," she said, marching up to where he and Aaron were standing.

"Yes, Ma'am." Despite being a good foot taller than her, Reid was visibly submissive in her presence. Jillian had no doubt this was his boss, the woman in charge.

"Where's the girl?" the woman asked, surveying the scene.

Reid pointed at the car, and Jillian came out trembling, wondering if she was in trouble too. But as the woman approached, Jillian could see her stoic face softening.

"You must be Jillian Sandro." Jillian nodded. "I'm Director Rollins," she said, quickly flashing a badge. "I understand you've been through quite an ordeal."

Jillian nodded again and Director Rollins snapped her finger. A man rushed over.

"This is Brent Riker," said Rollins. "He's going to drive you back to headquarter, where you'll give your statement, and then we have some paperwork we're going to need you to fill out."

"What about Reid?" Jillian asked.

"Agent Jackson will be along shortly."

Jillian reluctantly climbed into the back seat of the sedan with Rollins's lackey and as they were driven away, she turned back to watch the whole scene shrink away.

CHAPTER ELEVEN

After telling Riker everything that had happened, he asked her to write it down. Then asked her to tell him again as he went over it.

"Just being thorough," he told her.

A lot of questions about Reid's involvement were asked, and Jillian began to wonder how much trouble he was in.

When he was finally done with the interrogating, Riker brought in a lawyer who sat down next to Jillian with a non-disclosure agreement. They assured her she could go home as soon as she signed it, but also politely explained what the consequences would be if she breathed a word of the agency's involvement to anyone outside of the agency. There was no hesitation. She wanted to forget about it all as much as they did.

Riker and the lawyer left as Director Rollins

walked in with another gentleman who wasn't dressed nearly as sharply as everyone else.

"We thank you for your cooperation, Ms. Sandro," she said. "Agent Gavin Maxwell here will escort you home. If we need anything else, we know how to reach you." She turned on her heel and left.

That was it, Jillian had been dismissed.

"If you'll follow me, Ms. Sandro," said Gavin.

They walked down the hall not far behind Rollins and as she entered another room, Jillian caught sight of Reid. Their eyes met for a second before Rollins shut the door behind her.

"What's going to happen to him?" she asked.

"Hard to say," Gavin said with a shrug.

Reid stared at the door for a few more seconds before turning his attention to Director Rollins.

"Where is Maxwell taking her?" he asked. "Ma'am," he added after seeing the icy expression on her face.

"Home."

Aaron kicked him from under the table, reminding him what he should be worried about right now.

"Now let's go over this one more time, gentleman," she said.

It was late when Director Rollins finally let Reid leave. He pulled into his driveway, feeling the familiar exhaustion, but immediately walked across the street to Jillian's house. As he stood on the front step listening to the doorbell echo through the house, he told himself that she had succumbed to fatigue and didn't hear, yet couldn't help feeling that she was simply avoiding him.

Deciding to try again first thing in the morning, he walked back to his house with both hands in his pockets. As he approached his darkened porch, Reid could just make out something, or someone, lying across the swing. He walked up to discover Jillian, fast asleep.

"Hey," he said, crouching close to her face and her eyes fluttered open. "What are you doing here?"

She sat up while he kept the swing steady. "I couldn't go inside."

"A team has already done a sweep," he said. "I promise there's no more surveillance equipment."

"That's not it," she said, shaking her head. "Even if they're not watching me, that was never my home. It wasn't even my father's, it was *his*."

"Come inside," Reid said, taking her hand. "It's chilly out here."

She nodded and let him lead her into the house. Her hand in his felt good and Reid resisted the temptation to pull her into him.

"I didn't know where else to go," she said. "All I have left is my aunt and I didn't know what to say." She stifled a sob. "How do I tell her that her brother-in-law was… What am I supposed to say to them?"

[145]

Reid wiped away a tear that was sliding down her cheek. "Of course you can stay here. I want you here with me."

"Thank you," she whispered.

"And we can worry later about what to say to everyone. You should get some sleep now. You're exhausted."

"Sleep does sound good."

She followed Reid upstairs and he found a t-shirt for her to sleep in.

"Will you stay here?" she asked as he pulled back the covers and she crawled into his bed. "Next to me?"

Reid stripped down to his boxers and slid in next to her.

"There's nowhere I need to be but right here," he said and she curled up into his arms.

"Reid?"

"Hmm…" he answered, gently stroking her back.

"I love you."

He kissed the top of her head. "I love you too."

Jillian woke the next morning to sunshine peeking into the bedroom and Reid's arms around her. For a precious moment, it was easy to pretend everything else had been a horrible nightmare. But then she saw the bruise on her arm and knew it had indeed been very real.

"Good morning," Reid said into her neck.

She rolled over to see the smile on his face and felt one growing on her own.

"Good morning."

"How'd you sleep?" he asked.

"Very well, thank you," she said propping up on her elbow to look down at him.

His smile faltered. "That's good. But don't be surprised if some memories spring up over the next few days."

"You'll be here to protect me from them, won't you?"

"I hope so."

Now her smile faded. "Are you in trouble?" she asked.

"Yes. But they haven't decided what to do with me. There's a hearing next week."

"I'm sorry," she said.

"I'm not," he said, caressing her face.

Jillian took the hand and kissed his palm. Without warning, Reid rolled her onto her back and she felt a charge as he straddled her.

"No matter what happens," he said, staring right into her eyes, "I'd do it all over again."

She arched up to meet his lips and kissed him.

For the past hour, Reid had been sitting at a table listening to the Disciplinary Board run through everything he, Jillian, and Aaron had told them, pointing out every wrong choice he had made along the way. This was not looking good for Reid.

"In light of recent events," one of the board members concluded and Reid prepared himself for the blow, "we still could not overlook your exemplary service to this agency and the fact that your actions led to the apprehension of a known terrorist. After one month's suspension without pay, you shall be reinstated to full active duty."

"Thank you, Ma'am," said Reid, hardly believing what they were saying.

"This hearing is adjourned."

Reid stood up and exited the conference room to find Jillian and Aaron seated on a bench.

"How did it go?" Aaron asked as he and Jillian both stood.

"One month's suspension," said Reid.

"Really? That's great!" Aaron gave him a hearty pat on the back.

"But I'm handing in my resignation this afternoon."

"What? Why would you do that?"

Reid looked at Jillian then back to Aaron, who looked pissed. He didn't expect him to understand.

"Because I don't feel I'll be able to carry out the missions to the best of my ability anymore."

Now Aaron looked at Jillian.

"This is your doing, isn't it?" he asked and Jillian's jaw dropped.

"I had no idea," she exclaimed.

"This decision is mine and mine alone," Reid said. "Don't blame her."

Aaron crossed his arms over his chest. Reid knew his partner well enough to know that he was trying not to blow up at them. Aaron opened his mouth, but before he could say anything, Riker rushed up to them.

"Rollins thought you should see this," he said, handing a letter to Aaron.

Aaron read it and Reid watched his jaw tense up even more.

"What is it?" Reid asked.

"Based on what Jillian told Riker," he said, "we think it was Morozov at the cabin before you arrived. But as always, there isn't enough to bring him in."

"What?" Reid and Jillian said together.

"His lawyers came in and said that everything was circumstantial," Riker explained.

"But he was there," Jillian cried. "He told me everything."

Reid put an arm around her and could feel her starting to shake. From fear or anger, he wasn't sure.

"Did he ever tell you his name?" Riker asked.

"Well, no."

"But she was on his god damn boat," said Reid. "We know that for a fact."

"Morozov admits that he let his cousin borrow his boat," said Riker, "but claims he had no knowledge what Casimir was doing with the vessel. It's your word against his. There's no hard evidence. The man didn't even leave any fingerprints at the cabin."

"But my father…" said Jillian.

"He's not talking," Riker told her. "I think he's too scared."

"I want to talk to him," she said.

"I'm not sure that's a good idea," said Riker.

"I think it's a great idea," Reid asked, "Why not? She's the one person he might listen to."

Riker rubbed his temple. "I suppose you're right. I'll go talk to Rollins."

"Should we be worried?" Reid asked as Riker walked away. And by we, he meant Jillian.

"I don't know," Aaron said with a frown. "He's just made a clean escape. I don't imagine him doing anything to jeopardize that. But somebody needs to take this bastard down and soon."

Aaron's phone went off, and Reid recognized the tone.

Aaron looked at it. "I have to go."

Reid nodded as Aaron rushed off.

"Now what?" Jillian asked with worry written all over her face.

"If I know Wells, he won't let this go. But that's not something you and I need to worry about anymore."

"Are you really resigning?" she asked.

"Yes."

"But why?"

"Because I don't want to be out there in the field worrying about you," he said. "Or know that you're here worrying about me."

"You don't have to quit because of me."

"I know. But I want to. It just feels like the right step."

Jillian tried to control the shaking in her hands as she sat in the stiff chair, waiting for her father to appear on the other side of the plexiglass. She hadn't seen or spoken to him since he'd been restrained at the cabin and wasn't sure if she wanted to now. But at the moment, he was the only one keeping Morozov out of jail.

The door buzzed and Jillian watched a guard bring her father in. The sight of him in orange overalls and chains around his hands and feet broke her heart. How could this be the same man who had chased away her nightmares when she was a little girl?

His face brightened at the sight of her, but the smile only accentuated the sallowness. Had he aged that much in the last week, or had she simply not noticed before? The burden of his guilt must have taken its toll on him over the years.

"*Tesoro*," he said into the phone that enabled them to communicate across the barrier. "They didn't tell me who my visitor was. It's so good to see your face!"

"Why won't you tell them it was Morozov you were working for?"

He closed his eyes and shook his head.

"I can't," he said.

"I don't understand," she said. "What could you possibly have to gain by saying nothing?"

"I do it for you, to protect you!"

"But if Morozov is behind bars, what is there to worry about?"

Again Jacob shook his head. "The man is too smart. Even if he went to jail, someone in his family may come after you. I can't risk that."

"So you would rather rot in jail."

"It is to protect you," he said. "I love you, Jillian."

Her eyes stung from the tears threatening to break free, but Jillian refused to cry here for him.

"I loved the man you were before mother died," she said. "Now, you're just a coward."

She hung up as her father began sobbing, but she couldn't hear it, could only see his body shaking while he buried his head in his hands. The guard took him away as she exited the visiting area to where Reid was waiting for her by the sign-in desk.

"Will he talk?" he asked.

Jillian shook her head.

"It was worth a shot, right?"

She shrugged as they walked out to Reid's SUV. He let her sit in silence on the ride home. As they neared Renton, a thought struck her.

"I can't stay here anymore."

"What?" he asked. "Stay where?"

"*Here*. In Renton, in Washington. I need to make a fresh start somewhere else."

She looked at him, wondering what his reaction would be. He continued to stare at the road in front of them, his brows knitted together more in thought than a frown, or at least that what she hoped.

"I understand," he said, slowly nodding.

"You do?" she asked. Was this it? Were they breaking up, after everything they had been though?

"Yes," he said, reaching across for her hand. "But I hope you realize I won't let you do it alone."

"Really?" Jillian could feel the smile forming on her face. "You'd come with me?"

They stopped at a red light and Reid looked right at her. "You're the only thing keeping me here, Jillian. If you're ready for a fresh start, then so am I."

Two weeks later Reid was loading the last of the boxes into a moving truck when Aaron pulled up on his motorcycle.

Reid set the box down and walked over to greet his friend, who he hadn't spoken to since turning in his resignation.

"You weren't going to leave without saying goodbye, were you?" Aaron asked.

"I wasn't sure you were speaking to me."

Aaron's fingers fidgeted with the strap of his helmet.

"So Denver, huh?"

"It was the one place that appealed to us both," said Reid.

"I hear they have a great football team."

"Don't tell Jillian that," Reid laughed.

"You sure she's worth it?" Aaron asked.

"Without a doubt."

As if on cue, Jillian walked out carrying a box. She dropped it by the others and joined the two men.

"Hey," she said.

"I couldn't let Jackson here leave without saying goodbye."

"Of course," she smiled.

Aaron stared down at his feet awkwardly before pulling Reid into a big bear hug.

"Good luck, man. I'm going to miss you."

"Same here, Wells."

Aaron let him go and after hesitating, pulled Jillian into a hug. She looked as surprised as Reid was.

"Take care of him," Aaron told her. "And call me if you guys ever need anything."

"I will," she said.

Aaron stepped back, gave Reid one last handshake, and climbed back onto his bike.

Reid put his arm around Jillian as they watched him ride off.

"Are you okay?" Jillian asked and Reid looked down into her warm brown eyes.

"Absolutely. Are you ready for our next adventure?"

Her face broke into the same huge grin he fell in love with at the falls. "Absolutely."

CHAPTER TWELVE

Aaron Wells sat at the stainless steel table where Casimir was already seated and handcuffed to a bolted metal bar.

"To what do I owe this pleasure?" Casimir asked with a smirk.

"You look pretty smug for a guy who is going to rot in prison," Aaron said.

Casimir shrugged. "If you are here, then I must have something you want."

"I want to know who your buyer is."

"What makes you so sure I had a buyer?" Casimir asked.

"Because we both know you're in it for the profit," said Aaron. "Why risk everything if you didn't have some someone ready to fork over the cash?"

When Casimir didn't respond, Aaron

continued talking.

"Jillian Sandro said there was someone else on the boat. Someone reminding you not to fuck this up." Casimir flinched when he said this. "Who was he? Was that your buyer?"

"Unless you have something to offer me," Casimir sighed, "then we are done here."

"Who gave up Reid Jackson's name? Is it someone in the agency?"

Casimir shrugged. "I never bothered to ask."

"What about your cousin, Morozov?" Aaron asked. "Maybe we can get him to talk."

This made Casimir laugh. "Good luck with that. He is even better protected than I."

"We'll just have to see about that," Aaron said as he stood, signaling for the guard to let him out. "Hope you enjoy prison food."

As Aaron walked back out to his car, he couldn't help feeling disappointed, even though he hadn't really expected Casimir to give anything up. Hopefully he'd have better luck with Aleksandr Morozov.

Don't Miss

No Way Out

The Second Book in the Love & Lies Series

When Aaron Wells finds an unlikely ally in
Aleksandr Morozov's wife, he begins to question
Clara's motives, and his own judgment.

Available June 2015

Also available by Alex Strong

Island Runaway

Acknowledgments

Being an independent author means I did this book all by myself, right? That couldn't be further from the truth. This book wouldn't be half as good without the support of many people. First I have to thank Cattigan for all her work on this series and helping me to see hidden sub-plots that did not help the story, but they sure were good for a laugh! Thanks again to my cheer squad, Andrea, Liz, and Tama, for believing in me and making me feel like I can pull this off. Thank you to Luke L. for helping to fix my mistakes and your invaluable input not just on this book, but the last one as well. I also want to acknowledge my friends and fellow writers from the Eastside RWA group. I have learned, and continue to learn, so much since becoming a member. And a big thank you as always to my supportive husband for shamelessly promoting my work to his friends and colleagues. I love you!

About the Author

Alex Strong has loved stories, whether she's reading them or telling them, since she was very young. But it wasn't until after the birth of her youngest son that she realized what she wanted to do most was be an author. Her past lives include working as a waitress, a sales clerk, and a nanny. Though she has been all around the world, including two years living in the Philippines as a child, Alex is proud to call the Pacific Northwest her home and lives in the Seattle suburbs with her husband, their two boys, and two fluffy dogs.

Stay In Touch
Alexstrongwrites.com
Facebook.com/AlexStrongWrites
@TheAlex_Strong